THE CHRONICLES OF THE OBSCURE DETECTIVE

AMIR JOY

ISBN HARDBACK: 978-1-7356508-3-8
ISBN EBOOK: 978-1-7356508-4-5
ISBN PAPERBACK: 978-1-7356508-5-2
For more information, visit:
www.amirjoy.net

The author wishes to express his gratitude to the late
Sir Arthur Conan Doyle, but for whom this book could
never have been thought, let alone written…

CONTENTS

EPISODE I:
VAGUENESS

Inspector Said I, 'I'm dejected in saying this, but, if Mr Holmes was to be solving this case with us, he would have been, unquestionably, downhearted upon us.'

'Why would you say so?' asked the prefect, crossly.

'For we have, unfortunately, committed some gaffes which he had forewarned us about umpteen times.'

'And what may those gaffes be?' asked the prefect, sardonically.

'Well', I answered, 'For your case, I quite expect him to criticise you by saying "*It is a capital mistake to theorise before one has data.*" While for my case he would, undeniably, say "*The more outré and grotesque an incident is the more carefully it dese—*"'

As I was about to finish writing my little escapade, I was interrupted by two knocks on my flat's door, followed by a third one after a couple of seconds. 'Yes, Mr Vandican, pray, come in.' I cried.

While passing through the door, he remarked, 'B-but… How did y—?'

'Oh, please, Mr Vandican, ask yourself this query.' I implied while watching him stand in front of the door for a couple of seconds. Lost in the thought of his query, he eventually said while having a disheartened look upon his face, 'It was my knocking on the door. How could I have been so slow-witted?'

'For, as Mr Holmes once told Watson, "*you see, but you do not observe. The distinction is clear*".'

'Yes, I comprehend, but it really isn't that simple for ordinary people like myself', he complained as he took a seat on the settee.

'A mind without exercise is just like a body without exercise, my friend. If you halt training your grey cells, as M. Poirot baptized them, I'm afraid they will tarnish', I replied.

'Can you really train your mind? How do you even accomplish that?' asked my companion.

'By enhancing your engrossment and ratiocination. You need to perceive things that you do not customarily do. Train your mind to start noticing and observing what your eyes see. Seeing is just the first step to reason. You ought to use your five senses if essential and, most importantly, to put yourself in the place of your subject. For the sake of elucidating this argument, I shall apply them for your convenience.'

'Pray, do so.'

'When you first entered the room, I observed three things out of your common physical appearance. These three things distinguished what you have been doing so far this morning.

'This morning you wore your pince-nez and did a great amount of reading, you did some manual labour that, most likely, was washing the dishes, and you've been to the floristry to give Stevie your pot of flowers.'

'I know you've meant to see and observe things sir, but by George! I do not even know how you deduced these things, and I am your subject. Please explain!' pleaded my companion with excitement.

'My dear friend, I am certain you would see it as a simple matter once explained. You see, you did a great amount of reading, for the pince-nez left its mark on your nose. I instantaneously asked myself, in what circumstances would a pince-nez leave a mark? Obviously, the first notion that came to my mind was after doing a great amount of reading. That is the first deduction. The second was that you washed the dish... Mr Vandican, you can think about my analysis after I finish it' said I as I saw my companion losing his engrossment and thinking about my first analysis.

'I'm sorry, I didn't mean to do that. Pray, recommence, you have my full concentration.'

'You washed the dishes for your chemise has crumples that start from your elbows. Obviously, I used the same method I had used in the first deduction and realized that these kinds of crumples only happens when one folds his chemise until his elbows. The Most common reason for this action is doing manual labour. I asked myself afterwards, what sort of manual labour would my companion do? There were some other probabilities other than washing the dishes, but washing the dishes was the most probable assumption. Lastly, you went to the floristry for I can smell the natural scent of flowers attached to you. You have given Stevie your pot of flowers for I can see a slight stain of potting mixture on your chemise just below your chest. In what circumstances would the potting mixture stain that part of the body? The only explanation that works with the fact that you have been to the floristry is that you carried the pot of flowers to the floristry, and on your way there, you stained your chemise with potting mixture. Bear in mind, these deductions were deemed in a matter of seconds for my mind is quite trained' I elucidated lastly.

As you may have been accustomed to my friend's habit, he sat silently thinking about the analysis when he finally remarked, 'My friend, you're truly Mr Holmes' Acolyte. I cannot imagine the amount of training you have done to achieve this kind of intellect. Will I achieve the same intellect as yourself upon training my mind?' my companion asked with some excitement.

'For a matter of fact, yes, you can achieve this kind of intellect by training your mind, but at any rate', I asked, 'Do you need any aid with something else?'

'No-no sir, I just came to give you the newspaper as usual.' he said.

'Appreciated.'

Some minutes had passed since any of us had said a word. I was completing my modest escapade while he, being like a child watching his tutor, observed me while I was writing.

'Have you finished your monograph about Mr Holmes's techniques?' he asked.

'Oh, the monograph, yes...' I answered, 'I'm afraid that it's still far from being finished, but it will be at some point. As an alternative, I am recording our last week's adventure.'

'Inspectors should find another job if we stick around for too long.' He remarked while giving a chuckle.

I gave out a slight titter. 'I pray they find their upcoming cases demanding for without subjects to work on I can't complete the monograph', I said, fretfully.

'Looking back at how you were able to solve the mystery that puzzled all the yard, they might consult you regularly just as they did with Mr Holmes', he suggested.

'Don't amplify me, Mr Holmes was on a league of his own. If he were your adversary in a game of chess, he would have been several steps ahead of you. That is what he was like. And what scares me the most about him, but at the same time I admire, is that by a mere glimpse at you, in an instant, he can make out your background and more importantly your feeble point.'

'Well well', he said, 'If you can't be him, you can be his second. But I can assure you, sir, by how you induced last week's mystery, that you have a sophisticated mind, unlike the typical mind.'

'Really, I did nothing. Its mere observation and reasoning, nothing more nothing less.'

'Once a man sticks a notion to his mind, nothing can change it but himself. In any case, here is your newspaper sir. I will be in my usual place if you need anything', he said, while handing me the newspaper and walking towards the door.

'Mr Vandican, pray, come back. I need your aid in a minor matter', I asked while watching his figure turning to sit back on the settee.

'Absolutely, how can I aid you?'

'Can you remind me of some of the details about Mr Terry's case, which I fail to remember, and I highly need it for finalizing my escapade?

Before we resume upon this part, my esteemed readers, I believe you are in total vagueness about the present affairs, thence, I would like to recall some events, while providing, a brief chronicle lecture, so that you can fully comprehend the, at present...

EPISODE II:
A CHRONICLE BEHIND THE IDOLISATION

As a reasoner and an acolyte of Mr Holmes' methodology and way of contemplating, I do not believe in providence. Every being has his circumstances and varied intelligence, thence, these are reasons that a being can change his own providence by his own hand.

For instance, a man is condemned to have 20 years of jail, and all the evidence is against him. But then, the convicted attorney appeared, changing the case upside down by making the convicted man innocent. Is it providence that made this convict innocent? The notion is rejected for the fact that a third party appeared persuading the jury's decision by his intellect.

What if a man is a professional boxer? At his debut match, he won by a KO and was determined that he is proficient enough for taking up the champion. He then boxed the champion and ended his own career by breaking his eye socket. Is it providence that this miserable thing occurred to him? The notion is rejected, again, for after he won his debut, ego made him overconfident, thinking that he can outbox the champion without enough experience. What were the consequences of his ego? The end of his career, as mere as that.

Nevertheless, I know it's wry, but as people say, I was fated to have my mother die six years after my birth. Hence, my father bore her responsibility and took adoring care of me. He was a sailor. Thus, I travelled with him to Western Europe for that was our line of work. We were not that prosperous for me to attend a private school, but from an early age, my father purchased plenty of books for me to educate myself from. Amid these books were Dr Watson's adventures and biographies of Mr Holmes. From there, I was fortunate enough to study his methods. Another great detective I discovered, that did the exact same thing to his companion as Mr Holmes did to Dr Watson, and that was to read his mind by mere reasoning, was C August Dupin. Unfortunately, he was a fictional character written by Edgar Alan Poe. In any case, the subjects of the books my father acquired varied from literature to grammar to mathematics, and other subjects. To be more synopsis, I was home studying.

After saving enough money, I decided to follow my aspiration to study and examine Mr Holmes's methodology. It was laborious, but, for my goal's sake, I departed from my father in London. Primarily, it was strange, in a way, to walk on steady land for living in a vessel, most of your life will be different from living on steady land. Nevertheless, I got the hang of it and had two errands, in my mind, to attain. The first one was to proceed to 221b Baker Street and observe Mr Holmes' place of work, study, and daily life. In other words, I wanted to observe the scene of induction, where his magnum opus was occurring. I was eagerly anticipating the day I would behold at a place where the magnum opus was occurring.

The second one was to promptly make a name for myself around London in solving anonymities and criminalities, for, my train of thought ran as so:

[1] I would solve a crime that the yard is incapable of solving.

[2] By solving that mystery, I would make a name for myself.

[3] By making a name for myself, the yard and the people would consult me more often making me a part-time consulting detective.

[4] By being a consultant and having subjects to work on, I have hence, enough material to help me use Mr Holmes methods and write a monograph about his methods.

Making up my mind, I, hence, went straight to 221b Baker Street in the hope of beholding at Mr Holmes's room. Arriving at Baker Street and heading to my destination, I was smelling a rosy scent. Looking to my right, I perceived a floristry across the street full of flowers with dissimilar colours among them that varied from redish to yellowish and to many other iridescent colours. But having my eyesight particularly on the velvet flowers, for they were the residence of this rosy scent I had smelled. These velvet flowers go by the name of hybrid tea roses, also known as Mister Lincoln, and produce a classic rosy fragrance that could be smelled from fifteen feet away.

Anyhow, returning to the main point, I arrived at the front of the door. Upon observing the rusted metal "221b" figures written on the door, my heart commenced racing with excitement at that moment as if I'm about to have my debut boxing match. All I was thinking about was that I would finally, after long anticipation, be able to behold the workplace I have imagined various times.

I rang the bell and waited for someone to answer. Between this interval, I thought I had waited one hour eagerly for the opening of the door when, in fact, only ten or so seconds had passed. After beholding my life in a flash, the door, to my relief, had finally opened.

EPISODE III:
MR RICHARD VANDICAN

As the door opened, I saw a tall milky skinned, muscular being, beholding earnestly at the chap in front of him. With his sharp, nutty eyes, oblong face with a high forehead and cheekbones, aquiline nose, and inky black parted hair standing behind the door, 'May I be your aid with something young man?' asked the man while beholding me with his sharp eyes.

'Is the flat that Mr Sherlock Holmes occupied in his days occupied?' I asked eagerly. 'If it is, may you ask the renter for a mere ten minutes of his time so that I could observe the workplace of Mr Holmes?'

'Oh, I see now. Pray, come in', he answered.

He walked in front of me as I was following him as if I was a tourist following his guide. As we entered the sitting-room, he pointed to an armchair so that I would sit on it. 'Just a couple of minutes, sir. I will go get two cups of tea', he said. After a couple of minutes, he was back with the warm tea. 'It seems that you are a Sherlockian', he said while giving a gentle beam.

'Anyone would be an admirer of an intellectuality that comes once every generation. If people would just understand his magnum opus', I implied.

'Quite so', he said. 'My name is Richard Vandican, the landlord, and I'm honoured to meet a fellow Sherlockian besides myself.' He introduced himself while stretching his arm out so that we shake hands.

'My name is Williams Joy. Glad and honoured too, sir.'

'Well Mr Joy, I'm just prying if you can indeed deduce like Mr Holmes. What do you observe about me?' he asked with an eager face. Fortunately, it wasn't the first time for me to try Mr Holmes' Methods, so I was somehow used to using them. I observed Mr Vandican, for a couple of seconds, and remarked 'Fair enough, I will start with the obvious observations first.'

'You're, sir, a heavy smoker, left-handed, and obviously not British but you're speaking English fluently, so most probably you're either Australian or an American living in England for some time.'

'Astounding!' he cried, 'pray, continue.'

'You're a sailor who had, most likely, been to France and your line of work was in the western European region working on a vessel by the name of "Macdonough". One of your hobbies is fishing, and lastly, I am sorry for your loss. It seems that your wife has died recently.'

'Mr Joy...I am truly lost for words! Tha-that was brilliant! Everything was correct! Pray! Elucidate your reasoning.'

'Well enough, let us start with the heavy smoking. The ashes in the ashtray on the table could make up, judging by its size, more than seven tobaccos. All of which are of the same kind. And by the look of things in the house you are a bachelor. As such, the tobacco should be yours and you're the one who smoked it and by the looks of the ash, they have obviously been smoked today.'

'You're obviously not British judging by your accent. Unfortunately, I have not gotten the chance to converse with someone speaking either Australian or American, that is why I suggested both. Due to the fact that you are wearing a sailor's outfit and that one of the crew members in the photograph on the shelf, has the same features as yourself, show, sir, that you are a sailor. I am a sailor myself and, on the photograph, the name of the ship is visible and coincidentally, I was also working in the western European region and heard the names of some of the other vessels working on the same line as well. I was providential that yours was one of them.'

'You have been to France for the ashtray isn't an ordinary English one, and the words fabriqué en France are engraved on the side.'

'Your right thumb has scratches made by what seems to be something like a hook… made when you tried hooking the fish bait on it. The scent of fresh fish can be smelled from the kitchen, and the pile of boxes near the door were tightened by an obvious fishing knot called "The Blood Knot", and so your hobby is observably fishing.'

'A-Astounding, sir! Marvellous!' He exclaimed with wildly excited eyes.

'To conclude, one of the boxes was opened, and I managed to take a glimpse of garments that looked like that of a woman's. Combining that with the unkempt ness of the room, your dishevelled state, and the ring you are wearing, enlightened me about your wife's death that happened recently', I elucidated lastly.

'Magnificent! Everything is so easily comprehended now!'

'You remind me of Dr Watson. I'm sure if Mr Holmes was here, he would've told you *"Every problem becomes very childish when once it is explained to you"*, I implied while trying my best to imitate Mr Holmes. He gave a chuckle expressing his amusement and said, 'Quite so. Anyhow, there is just one thing you may have forgotten. How did you know I'm left-handed?' He asked eagerly while bending his back so that he gets closer.

'Well, Mr Vandican, I find it satirical that you are asking this query while holding your tea with your dominant hand. Nevertheless, the scratches on your right thumb show that you were obviously holding the hook with your dominant hand at the time while hooking the food with your scratched hand. That should be it', I answered lastly, giving a puff of air after inhaling.

Mr Vandican was at that time lost in his thoughts whle gazing at the cup of tea lost in thought, possibly thinking of his vacuous query. When he finally came back to himself, he exclaimed with a big beam on his oblong face, 'You are the man I was waiting for, Mr Joy. You are greatly welcomed to stay in 221b Baker Street.' At that time, my mind was capering with joy. I did not believe that I would have a chance to live in the same place in which the man whom I have the greatest respect for lived. But the first part of what he said had puzzled me a little. 'What do you mean, sir, by, "The man I was waiting for?" I asked in attentiveness.

'Its…' He started saying but paused, gazing at the floor for several minutes while taking sips of tea. 'Making up my mind, sir, there is no harm answering your query in the form of a tiny tale', he said. With the lack of concern for my response, he preceded to his tale.

'As you have propounded earlier, I am indeed Australian. I have indeed been working as a sailor in the Macdonough Vessel. I married an Australian Dame, and we have both perceived Mr Sherlock Holmes as the white chevalier of justice.'

'Her dream has always been to come to London and live in 221b where Mr Holmes had once lived. As any husband would try to make his wife's dream a reality, I made some enquiries from the various voyages I made as a sailor in London, and I've finally, after some dialogue, come to a manageable price for this house with the previous landlord. After we settled down some years ago, we decided to only rent Mr Holmes's flat for someone who deserves it. We have waited but nobody with the intellect we looked for had arrived, with the anomaly of today.'

'Unfortunately, my wife died a week ago. She would have been exceedingly radiant in seeing what you are capable of… that's my little tale.'

'And a fairly interesting one', I remarked.

We continued to converse on other topics that shared our interest until we realized that several hours have passed, the moon's eye was the only enlightenment at the time. 'I'm sorry to keep you up, it's getting late, and you seem tired. Let me show you to Mr Holmes' room.' he said, arising from his seat while stretching his muscles.

'Not at all, it was an interesting conversation, sir.' I said, getting up and following Mr Vandican to the stairs.

'The room is the one to your left upon entering the sitting-room', he elucidated. 'Roger that, good night' I said, escalating the stairs.

'Good night, sir'

...

EPISODE IV:

SCENE OF INDUCTION:

WHERE THE MAGNUM OPUS TOOK PLACE

Mounting the stairs, I was enumerating each step until the seventeenth one as mentioned by Mr Holmes. I was then in front of the sitting-room door. I took some quick breaths to sedate my heartbeats. "I finally made it. At last..." was the thought that kept running through my mind. I took the confidence breath, widened my eyes, and opened the door.

The first thing I noticed upon entering was the scent of tobacco. Instinctively, my eyesight turned to the Persian slipper where Mr Holmes kept his tobacco and on the right side of the sofa where he used to keep his pipe rack. Widening my sight, I saw the room lucidly. Unfastidious with the mark of scintillation, just as I imagined the room to be. I felt strange for a couple of seconds for regarding the flat I'm going to live in as a museum. Nevertheless, I took a tour of the sitting-room starting from the broad bow window, the one facing Baker Street, and lunged from one nook to another. For reference, I tried my best to make a sprightly illustration of the sitting-room.

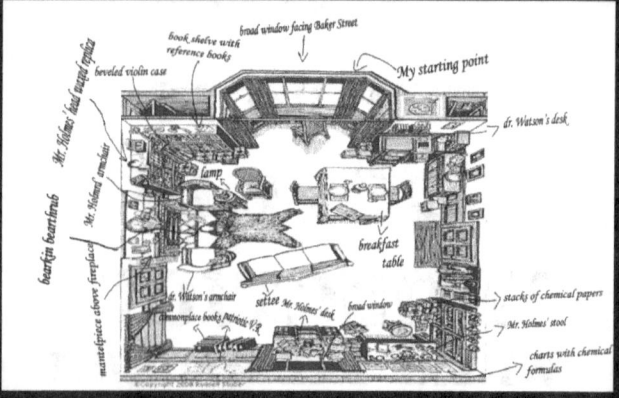

Moving to the left, the first thing I beheld at were the reference books that Mr Holmes used as an encyclopedia next to the mantelpiece. Raising my pointing finger to the books' names, I started reading them one by one. I began from A on the left side of the bookshelf. As I moved to the right, I was astounded by the sight in front of me. I took a step backwards from the astonishment! I could feel my heartbeat at that moment, trying to break through my ribs! It was Mr Holmes' head above the shelf! I took a step forward to look with closure at the figure and realized it was his wax replica of himself. Remembering one of Mr Holmes' cases named the Mazarin Stone, I, then, saw how Count Negretto Sylvius and myself had a comparable episode being fooled by Mr Holmes' wax replica.

Composing myself, I resumed going through the books. Halfway through the task, my attention altered from the reference books to the bevelled violin case in the corner. I always desired to acquire the ability to play the violin, and of course, to feel the engrossment of one's mind to a matter using a specific action to achieve full engrossment, as Mr Holmes was doing.

Resuming my tour and moving to the left, in a circular motion around the room, I gazed at the cocaine bottle, the photograph of Ms Irene Adler, the only woman which Mr Holmes esteemed, and the unanswered correspondence transfixed by a jack-knife in the middle of the mantelpiece. Moving towards it, I ran into Mr Holmes' armchair! The impact affected the lamp next to the armchair, and it began to lose balance! My mind was in a muddled and sceptical state. How could I have been so woolgathered!? Will I have enough time to catch the lamp before it plummets? These were the queries mingling through my mind while trying to reach for the lamp as it loses its balance and begins to tumble. I stretched my hand far enough so that I can catch it if it tumbles, but fortunately, it didn't get enough impetus for it to do so.

Self-constituting myself for a second time, I recommenced the tour. Pacing beside the lamp, I acquired some paces forward, and I could feel that I suddenly stepped on some sort of carpet. Looking downwards, I gawked at the sight of a bearskin facing the mantelpiece above the fireplace. To the right of the bearskin, the Persian slipper, which I cited earlier, was placed. To the left of the bearskin was Dr Watson's armchair, placed face to face with Mr Holmes' Armchair. To the left, beside the bearskin or to the right of Dr Watson's armchair, if I am seated, was the pipe rack which I also cited earlier. In the middle of the room was the settee. It was verging on two meters in length. Before I moved any further, I immediately sat in Mr Holmes' Armchair. I raised my legs and wrapped my hands around my knees, making my rectus femoris touch my epigastric abdominal region and my pectoralis major. In other words, making my thighs touch my upper abdomen and lower thorax or chest; curling myself up in the armchair just as Mr Holmes did when solving the red-headed league case in fifty minutes sitting this posture, smoking his three pipes. After giving myself this delectation, I rose up and carried on with the tour. I know I may have behaved like a juvenile but seeing one's idol's workplace and works is ineffable and celestial.

Reverting to the main point, the settee in the middle of the room was, I believe, one-fourth of a meter from Dr Watson's armchair. I had to squeeze myself to pass through the gap. Walking forward, I could see ahead of my sight the letters "V.R." on the wall. They were the patriotic "V.R.", which stands for Victoria Regina, Latin for Queen, done by bullets in packs opposite to Mr Holmes armchair. His alleged reason for shooting the bullets on the wall was because he was bored to death. Nevertheless, beneath the holes were commonplace books stacked above each other. There were at least ten manuscripts there. To the left of them was Mr Holmes' Desk, facing the broad window. Next to the desk was his stool, perpendicular to the acid-charred bench of chemicals. Above the bench, I could see chemical formulas, but I did not fathom what was written on them for I am not an expert in this field.

Turning to the left, a shelf was beside the bench. It was full of chemicals, presumably, flasks full of chemicals. I am not fully erudite with chemistry thence do not magistrate me by saying flasks for there were other types of flasks which I am not quite knowledgeable of their contents. On the ground, ahead of the shelves, were stacks of papers. Alas, I did not understand what was written; thus, my instinct told me it was chemistry. Moving forward, I beheld the breakfast table. Facing it from the side was, I believe, Dr Watson's desk. The first thing my eyes set on was the framed picture of General Gordon. Seeing it, my train of thought took me instinctively to glance at the unframed portrait of Henry Ward Beecher.

For readers, asking themselves the query, 'Why would my train of thought take me to the unframed picture?' The response is that in one of Dr Watson's stories, probably *The Cardboard Box*, an episode occurs between Mr Holmes and Dr Watson involving these two pictures. Mr Holmes deduces Dr Watson's train of thought by how Dr Watson looked from one photograph to another.

I opened Dr Watson's desk's drawer looking for his revolver. Predictably, it was not at hand. Altering my vision upwards, I beheld the petite bookshelf of medical books. 'Now I can dilate my knowledge furthermore', was my thought gazing at them.

By this I have completed the tour I awaited for so long. Standing in front of the broad bow window, the one facing Baker Street, watching the lights on the street. Nearly no hominid was on the street, save a couple reckoned on the hand. This day will be remembered, I kept saying to myself beholding the street. I have carried out my first task. Now I ought to get through with the other. As my consciousness was fading away from the lack of sleep, I lacked the power and ability to enter Mr Holmes' Bedroom, hence, gazing at the settee, I walked straight to it with the slight consciousness I had left.

EPISODE V:

THE DYING DETECTIVE

A week had passed since my arrival to 221b Baker Street, and I might say that, at first, I considered it a chimaera, but I may as well say, like most Homo sapiens do, "I'm living my dream".' Howbeit, it was a quotidian Saturday like any other. What I didn't know at that time was that it was this day that made a consequential change upon my life and was the initial point of my pilgrimage.

I had woken up that day early in the morning at about half-past eight. I had done my morning routine in addition to eating breakfast, and at about quarter-past nine, I was accommodated in Mr Holmes' desk resuming my monograph about Mr Holmes' methodology.

Some minutes had past, when I was interrupted by the pounding on the door, 'Come in', I said. Mr Vandican had opened the door slowly, which caused it to roar its squeaky noise. 'The newspaper, sir, as usual', he uttered, coming into the room.

'Cheers, my friend, prie, asseyez-vous', I said as I gestured to him with my hand to take a seat.

'Oh. No thanks are needed, sir. May this be the monograph, which you had informed me about the other day?' He asked while handing the newspaper and taking a seat in the armchair.

'Your instincts are on point, but I didn't start it yet. These are mere points which I would like to address in the monograph. One of the points I would like to address is how Mr Holmes uses Aristotle's Ratiocination, but before I answer the query, "how", I would like to tell you some chronicles about Aristotle's Ratiocination.'

'Please do so.'

'Firstly, Rationalism is the philosophy which holds that reason is the main source and test of knowledge, rather than experience. Mr Holmes was one of the most intelligent people who used this method. But, the origins of ratiocination run back in antiquity, initiating from the ancient Greek philosopher Aristotle. Aristotle rejected the central tenants of platonic, —which held that the observed or natural world was a mere approximation of an ideal world— works of his master, Pluto, and promoted the science of attaining deductions by mere observation. He applied this research across varied topics such as mathematics, physics, botany, politics and many other topics. Aristotle's approach was the weight of logic, based on reasoning and resulting from observation. Briefly, ratiocination. Aristotle's demonstrations of empirical logic had become central to most educational and scientific systems. Now that you know Aristotle's Ratiocination or Mr Holmes' methodology, I shall elucidate how he used it.'

'It seems, sir, that you know your history well.' Remarked my companion.

'Well, I have to say, I was fortunate enough to read about these topics in my early years.'

'I see now, in any case, pray, recommence.'

'Mr Holmes' most straightforward approach to a problem was deduction based on evidence, the logical thought that placed him several steps ahead of customary investigators. Mr Holmes often observes the little, but most essential, details that bare the whole case using ratiocination as his methodology. Mr Holmes can, hence, reason problems that others find most eccentric.'

'How did you find this brief history lecture?'

'Enjoyably knowledgeable. You amaze me with your knowledge, sir! But I'm fairly eager upon your answer to a certain matter.'

'What may this matter be?' I asked eagerly

'James Moriarty, "The greatest schemer of all time, the organiser of every devilry, the controlling brain of the underworld, a brain which might have made or marred the destiny of nations" as Mr Holmes described him to be. What is your take on him? I seldom hear you mentioning him', asked my companion with excitement that made his eyes sparkle. I thought for a moment about his query, and I eventually answered, 'To be honest, I don't know much about Moriarty. Mr Holmes took most of my time, and I didn't give him a thought before.'

'That was not what I expected, but nevertheless, I thank you for sharing your knowledge. Now I comprehend where his methodology came from.' Replied my friend with disappointment.

'It was just a brief discussion. Anyhow, today you are the one choosing the topic.'

'Oh yes, I've been bewildered all night having to pick one from a treasure trove.'

I may add that it became customary for us, Mr Vandican and I, to pick up an escapade from Dr Watson's collection of biographies and discuss it between us. A person chooses a story a day and shall recall its events, but must change one or more thing in the story which the other person shall figure out.

'Yesterday's episode was "The Dancing Man" which you have chosen, and opportunely, I noticed the point added by yourself. Today's episode is "The Dying Detective", and I'm decently sanguine that you will not figure out the mistake', he declared with a smirk on his face.

'I will try', said I, preparing for his narrative by closing my eyes and distilling.

'The story goes that one foggy October day, Mrs Hudson calls Dr Watson with calamitous news by notifying him that death is at Mr Holmes' door. Dr Watson then rushes to Mr Holmes to become aware of his severe state. Mr Holmes alleges that a contagious tropical disease infected him while working on a case with the Chinese sailors at Rotherhithe. Dr Watson tries to examine Mr Holmes, but Mr Holmes defies him, insisting he stay back by saying that he is not qualified and is ill-informed of this type of disease. He suggests the one man that can help him is Culverton Smith, a planter and microbiologist visiting London from Sikurai. Furiously and enigmatically, Mr Holmes reprimands Dr Watson when he is about to touch a small ivory box on the mantelpiece.

Dr Watson, resentfully hurt and grieved by Mr Holmes grave state, rushes to the one man capable of helping his friend. Initially, Mr Smith was hesitant to let Dr Watson in, but Dr Watson made his way to Mr Smith. Promptly, Mr Smith illumines hearing about Mr Holmes state saying, "He is an amateur of crime, as I am for disease. For him, the villain, for me, the microbe", and lastly sympathised to call upon Mr Holmes.'

'Dr Watson, reminded by Mr Holmes' instructions of returning home alone, returns to 221b alone to hide behind Mr Holmes's bed upon his instructions. Upon Mr Smith's arrival to 221b and awareness of Mr Holmes's state, he confesses his crimes: sending the ivory box bobby trapped with a disease and murdering his nephew to secure a "reversion" by getting his hands on the nephew's property. Mr Holmes then asks Mr Smith for a tobacco, while taking a sip of water and notified Mr Smith about the inspector coming to apprehend him. Mr Holmes asks Dr Watson to show himself after Mr Smith's contradiction to Mr Holmes's evidence being nugatory. Mr Holmes's elucidates how he did not only hoodwink his nemesis but the closest to him as well. Mr Holmes pacifies Dr Watson by stating he had to delude him to make his strategy work while giving Dr Watson's medical talents their respect. He then explains how he had not eaten for three days and how he: dilated his pupils with Belladonna to imbue his eyes with "the brightness of a fever"; smeared Beeswax around his mouth, making him look like he has not had food nor water for days, and; rubbed petroleum jelly or Vaseline across his forehead to aggrandize his ghastly face.'

'And by this sir, I've finished my episode for the day.' Said my companion giving a smirk like the earlier one. 'So, have you pinpointed anything?' He asked with the confidence that I had no answer to.

'Ha-ha. My friend, you sure know how to narrate a story. Unfortunately for you, I have perused this story recently. You thought I would not notice?' As I said those words, his smirk started to fade 'Initially, it was in November, not in October.' My companion changed his sight to the floor to show his disappointment. 'Secondly, Mr Smith—' as I was saying the answer, it appeared that Mr Vandican could not hear it from the continuous echoing of the doorbell.

'I should open the door; it seems that something is off. Excuse me, sir', he said while opening the door and rushing downstairs. As I waited for him, I finally heard his footsteps mounting the stairs, but he was not alone. Wondering whom this visitor may be, the door opened, and I could see Mr Vandican, and behind him was a tubby acorn eyed and haired wary looking, young lad. 'There may be an incident, sir! A case!' cried Mr Vandican, showing signs of agitation.

'Pray, regain your composure and apprise the matter before me' I said, as I gestured for them to take a seat.

'Stevie is working at the floristry across the street. I have known him and Mr Charles, the floristry owner, for some time now. Stevie, I want you to recompose yourself and apprise Mr Joy, what you have told me downstairs.' Sweat was dripping just like rain from Stevie. It seemed that he came here running like a mad hound down the streets.

'U-uh it-it-s ho-horrible, sir, gruesome', cried the lad with his agitated and frightful voice. I saw the fear in his eyes. What sort of dreadful incident might cause this lad to shiver with dread? A query I was asking myself as I saw Stevie's state.

'Little lad, you're a man now. I want you to stand up for that position. Inhale and exhale some air, recall your events, and lay them with a plucky heart', I exclaimed.

'Ye-yes, sir. Understood.' The lad took his time. I could see a determined and bold eye that told me he had set his mind. 'Okay sir, the events run as so.'

'I have been working with Mr Charles for the past five months now. We customarily open the floristry at nine with the anomaly of Saturdays in which we open at ten. What sir? What is the reason for opening an hour later Saturdays? I do not know the reason for that for I never asked him, and I did not really give it a thought. Mr Charles is the one who opens the store for he keeps the keys with him, and he is seldom late. Today, sir, I arrived at ten as usual and waited for Mr Charles; I waited until half-past teni, but he still did not show up. I was flabbergasted for this had never happened before. The notion that he may have caught a cold and is unable to come came to my mind and, therefore, with this notion in my mind, I went to pay him a visit and see how he is doing. He rents a flat in 137l Lynemouth Street, which is a ten-minute walk from the floristry. I rang the bell as I arrived, and the landlord opened the door. Fortunately, he recognized me for Mr Charles had invited me once there. I hastily explained the situation, and he let me in. This is where the gruesome part is sir.'

'You did a superb job till now, pray, carry on with the same pace', I said, widening my ears to not let any detail skip them.

'I opened the door of his flat an-and…I found Mr Charles laying on the ground with his face. Wa-wait, I did not mention that the first thing I noticed, when I first entered the room, was another man lying on his back with a pale face and a horrible expression on it that expressed, clearly, his anguish! At that moment, fear opened its gates in my ribs, and I was completely motionless for some minutes until I realised that Mr Charles was also in the room but laying on his face.'

'Fear did not let me move another step forward and I at once closed the door, rushed downstairs, told the landlord that Mr Charles does not want to be disturbed, and rushed to the only person that came to my mind and that's Mr Vandican. These are the events, sir.'

'This is dreadful. We must hurry and go to Mr Charles for this might be a grotesque business we might be dealing with', said I, getting up from my seat and preparing myself for this escapade. 'Get ready, Mr Vandican; we don't want to waste any time. I want to study the room before we call the yard.'

'Roger that sir.' As I was wearing my outfit, my mind was cynically full of joy for I had never imagined I would have an adventure this soon. Although a person might be lifeless, and sorrow should be my sensation, instead and involuntarily, joy was. Five minutes later, we were on the side road, following our guide, to the place of the incident.

EPISODE VI:

THE 137L LYNEMOUTH STREET MYSTERY

We explained the situation to the landlord upon our arrival and rushed to Mr Charles' Flat. Upon our opening the door, gruesomeness grasped our hearts in its trap. I realised then how hard it must have been for this young man to express what he saw.

There were two figures on the floor near the breakfast table, laying on the ground side by side. The figure with its face on the ground must be Mr Charles as Stevie had stated earlier and the other figure was what gave us the chill. Its face was as pale as white chalk opening his mouth to its fullest showing signs of immense agony. Its eyes widely opened like an eagle watching its prey, but in this situation, being ironically the opposite. Its hands were wrapped around its throat showing that, most likely, it had been poisoned. The poison being obviously in the two broken wine glasses on the ground that were filled with wine before they were broken.

'Oh, good heavens! What is this!? Wh-what has happened in here!?', cried the landlord, taking some steps backwards from the shock of the scene.

'Sir, do not be agitated and keep your calm', I pleaded

I warned everyone to keep away from the room and to take off, at once, to call the yard with the anomaly of Mr Vandican, whom I asked to stay inside with me. We closed the doors behind us and started to investigate the room.

'If you notice anything peculiar, inform me. I will study the cadavers', I uttered approaching the two cadavers.

Upon my bending to examine both cadavers, there was a bitter smell surrounding them. Ignoring the smell, I raised both of their clothes to see their lividity state. There were recognisable signs of lividity on both cadavers. I pressed the afflicted area to see if the lividity was fixed, but it wasn't. That suggested that both men died after six o'clock in the morning, for now is quarter past eleven and lividity begins to fix usually after five hours. That was one factor.

Another crucial factor I perceived is that they were murdered with cyanide poisoning. Conventionally, a person's lividity would turn cherry red if he or she died normally, but if a person dies from cyanide poisoning, certain signs would be detectable: The lividity would turn pink, lips would lose their colour, nails would turn purple, and lastly, a bitter scent would be smelled. All these signs were detectible on the cadavers.

I looked inside the pocket of the deceased to see who he may be but didn't find anything to answer the query. To my bewilderment, Mr Vandican said, 'This man might be Mr Robert Anndy – Ande- oh yes, I remember, it was Robert Anderson. Mr Charles told me once that Mr Robert comes here every Saturday morning with a bottle of wine to eat breakfast with Mr Charles. What is their relationship do you ask? Oh, I don't know, did not ask him about that.'

I stood up, looked around the room to see if there is any sort of clue for this mystification. I did not find anything. Everything in the room was just as it should be. Wait… Halloo! What is this?

I must add that from the look of things in the flat and from Mr Charles outfit that Mr Charles was not a wealthy man. I Must add this point for my readers get my intention on the following.

There was another wine bottle in the room. One that was yet to be opened. It wasn't Mr Charles' wine, for it was an expensive type, so obviously it was Mr Robert's. But why bring two wine bottles? Where did this extra bottle come from? Who brought it here? Was it homicide-suicide? Was it double suicide? Was it homicide? Is the poison in the opened wine bottle? If so is it in the sealed one too? These queries echoed through my mind for they were the only clue I could see in the room. I explained then to Mr Vandican the situation with the wine bottles, and he expressed the same confusion. 'Remarkable, isn't it?' I remarked.

'Yes, this is some grotesque business. The amount of wine in the opened bottle shows that it was poured for two persons only. Thence, knowing that there was no one else in the room, implies that the poison is in the opened wine bottle on the breakfast table.'

'Interesting, interesting. Let us search the room to see if we can find the cyanide used.' I suggested but with no results found at the end.

The room was also neat and there were no signs of theft. I darted from a corner of the room to the other to see if I can find a clue. Alas, there was nothing peculiar. My mind then was set upon the idea that our clue is outside the house. 'Do not jump to conclusions; this may be murder-suicide. All the facts fit with the idea except for the sealed wine bottle. If he intended to murder Mr Charles and then commit suicide, why bring two bottles. Nevertheless, let's interrogate the landlord before the yard arrives then we can set out to Mr Roberts household to see if we can find an enlightenment to the case. If we happen to find the cyanide poisoning there, then it settles the case as murder-suicide', I remarked.

'For our luck, Mr Charles told me about Mr Robert and in the middle of his conversation informed me where he lives.'

'Guess luck is on our side', I remarked.

Some minutes afterwards, we were in the sitting-room, unquestionably locking the room before us so that no one can tamper with any of the evidence.

'So, Mr Landlord, did anyone else come here with Mr Robert between 6 and 11 a.m.?' I asked.

'Only Mr Robert came today. I believe he arrived some minutes past 7.'

'Did you get to notice what was he carrying inside his bag other than the wine bottle? asked Mr Vandican.

'Well sir, Mr Robert comes here every Saturday with a wine bottle, so I got used to this fact and did not take notice if there was anything else.'

'Try to remember sir.' I pleaded him 'Try to focus, was there more than one bottle of wine?'

'Uh-I think…. hum, I don't think I remember. I just didn't take notice of it for it was something usual.'

'Can't blame you for that, it's normal for humans to see and fail to observe, especially with customary stuff', I said.

'Did Mr Charles buy any wine the other day? Did you observe him carrying anything?'

'Well sir, Mr Charles has a duplicate key to the house, so he can come and go as he pleases. So maybe he came with one the other day, and I didn't see him.'

'Never mind the wine for now then.'

'I'm really sorry, sir.'

'Don't be. Now, did Mr Charles have any enemies? Anyone who hated him? I asked

'No sir, I don't think so. Mr Charles was a good man. I don't ever recall that he had any enemies.'

'What about this, Mr Robert, what business does he have with Mr Charles?' asked Mr Vandican

'I don't really know anything about them with the anomaly of the fact that they are old friends.'

'What makes you think they were good friends? Is it that he brings a wine every Saturday to chat with Mr Charles?'

'In addition to that, Mr Charles told me that they were old mates and I don't think he ever mentioned anything gruesome about him.'

'Do you know anything about Mr Robert? Did he have enemies?' I asked

'No, sir. I only know that he is a well-known wine trader.'

'Do you know what t—' alas, we ran out of time for the bell rang violently and the yard was, probably, the reason.

EPISODE VII:
L'INSPECTEUR
EN CHEF

An inspector came in with two police officers and Stevie. 'I'm inspector Gerard of Scotland yard. This chap came and told us that a murder had occurred in this house. Is it true?' asked the inspector.

'Yes, it is true. Two men have been murdered here to-day morning', answered Mr Vandican.

'I see, take me to the crime scene. W-wait, Vandican was it? Such a coincidence.'

Good lord Gerard! Good seeing you yet again old lad! How have you been? I see you are a prefect now. Nicely done old friend' Cried Mr Vandican while guiding the inspector to Mr Charles' Flat.

'Hold on, you two know each other?' I asked with a muddled face.

'Oh, we were flatmates back in the day', answered the inspector.

'That explains it', said I.

'By the way, this is Mr William Joy, Gerard. He was a detective in France and only came to England the past week.' He paused for a moment and then looked at me.

'N'est-ce pas vrai mon ami?' cried Mr Vandican. What was he talking about I didn't know, so I exclaimed my confusion?

'What are y…' He tapped me with his elbow as to say, "play your role".

'Oui, c'est correcte', I said, lastly.

'Is that so? Well, I would like to see what you are capable of. Said the inspector whilst looking at the door that Mr Vandican was about to open.

'Oh lord. It's a sickening sight.' Cried the inspector turning his head sideways and placing his hand on his mouth.'

'Yes. It is', replied one of the officers.

I explained to the inspector after his investigation of the room about our own investigation and what we had found. After studying the room, we went downstairs to the sitting-room. 'This business tells me that the only explanation is either murder-suicide or double suicide. There is no other explanation. No one was in the room with them and the man or Mr Robert as you say his name is, was the one who brought the wine', implied the inspector.

'Let's not theorise before we have enough evidence inspector', said I.

'Well, there isn't anyone capable of doing it except the landlord,' said the inspector.

'The landlord can't do it. Only Mr Robert owned the wine. The inquiry, therefore, is if he had the possession of the two bottles of wine', remarked Mr Vandican.

'Anyhow, Mr Vandican and I would like to have our own investigation if you may.'

'If you don't interfere with our work, then you are free to act as you wish.'

'Thank you, sir.'

'Well if it wasn't for my friend, Vandican, I wouldn't have agreed.' He exclaimed, giving a chuckle and looking at Mr Vandican.

'To show my thankfulness, I will tell you a clue', said I.

'Really' He replied looking at me earnestly while moving his ears towards my mouth 'What may this clue be may I ask?' I lowered my voice and approached him saying, 'The clue is outside this house!' He stepped backwards, showing his confusion and exclaimed, 'I thought you were being serious.'

'Don't get me wrong, I am serious.'

'I don't understand', he asked in bewilderment.

'You will, eventually. Anyhow, we, Mr Vandican and I, must leave for Westmoor for that's were Mr Robert' Household is. I am sure we will meet there some other time today. Good luck with the investigation' said I, lastly as we departed from 137l Lynmouth Street.

In half an hour, we were in the cab on our way to Westmoor. We seldom talked in the cab for we sat with our own thoughts about this perplexing case. I remembered that Mr Vandican told the prefect that I was a detective from France, so I thought of asking him for the reason.

'Is it customary for people to fib about their profession to inspectors?' I asked.

'What—oh, that— It was necessary for we would not have otherwise had a chance to be a part in this mystery.'

'Fair enough. That explains it. Je devrais prendre en français à partir de maintenant mon ami', Said I with a chuckle.

'Oui, mais pas trop, la cour peut comprendre', replied my companion, while giving a laugh.

'What do you make of the matter'? asked my companion.

'Well, we can't build bricks without clay as Mr Holmes would say.'

'But it is weird, isn't it? I mean, if we do not find the cyanide poisoning in Mr Robert's household, then its murder done by someone who knew the deceased well. I mean, if Mr Robert wanted to commit suicide, he wouldn't hide the cyanide poisoning.'

'That is what we are grounding on. If we don't find the cyanide poisoning, then it is inevitably murder made, as you have said, by someone familiar with the victims.'

After, I would say, 15-minutes, we perceived the shadow of mountains in the countryside, filled with diverse colours. As we approached the countryside even more, the shadow began to fade, and the green-coloured mountains took all our attention. Westmoor was filled with green nature. Every house had a considerable garden beside it. The houses, as I could perceive, were lined so that behind them were enormous farming fields and behind those fields were mountains full of trees till its climax. 'What a peaceful, imaginative sight. If I get to choose where to live my retirement days, I would certainly choose Westmoor,' remarked my companion, looking at the fields.

'I would perhaps do the same.'

After 5 minutes or so, we arrived at Westmoor. We asked the cabby if he knew where Mr Robert Anderson's household is. Alas, he did not know, so we had to ask through the houses in Westmoor until we had finally found the right house.

EPISODE VIII:
THE WESTMOOR
INTERROGATION

'If I knew that wine trading would give you this much, I would have probably changed careers a long time ago', remarked Mr Vandican while entering through the house's fence. It was an elegant house furnished with hundreds of flowers surrounding it.

We knocked on the door and immediately, a tall dark-haired, blue-eyed, and smooth-skinned maid opened for us.

'Mr Robert Anderson's household, sir. How can I help you?' Asked the maid, looking from one of us to another.

'Pardon us for the intrusion madam, but unfortunately, Mr Robert died this morning, and we are here to investigate', I said and promptly we could see the daze on her face.

'Co-come in', she said, as she took us to the sitting-room.

'Can you wait here? We would like to search the house, immediately, before someone tampers with anything. Announce that to your head of household. Mr Vandican, please go with her, afterwards, please come and show me where Mr Robert's room is', said I.

We at once rushed through the house searching for the cyanide bottle, entering all the rooms and searching for it. Shortly afterwards, the maid came to show me the room, but I was already in it. I searched everywhere starting from the drawers to his litter but did not find any trace of cyanide. I returned to the sitting-room waiting for Mr Vandican return with his results, but woefully he did not find anything.

'I searched his room upside down but with no results', I remarked. 'This settles it as murder, or maybe he concealed it somewhere else.'

'I think that that's a truncated possibility. If he was committing suicide, why bother to conceal the bottle? It must be murder', replied my companion.

'Indeed, I agree. But we did not find anything in the other rooms, and the head of household disapproves our entrance to her room', said I questionably

'Maybe she anticipated that we were searching for the missing', replied my companion

'It might be a possibility.'

'What about the other rooms?' Asked my companion?

'Did not find anything', I answered in disappointment.

'Perhaps the murderer anticipated our coming?'

'It remains a possi—', said I when abruptly, an alluring lady with reddish hair, a chisled jaw line, and anthracite eyes, rushed in the sitting-room with her eyes fixed upon us. Without giving us a moment to introduce ourselves, she instantaneously asked, 'Who did it? Who killed my beloved brother, and why did you rush through the house?' she asked with water drops preparing to drop on her face.

'Why do you assume that he was murdered? Was he a hated man? I asked, ignoring her last query.' The confusion was obvious on her face. She waited a few seconds and then said, 'no, the maid just told me that my brother died. I just assumed he was murdered for he is a healthy man. Did he die naturally? How did he die?'

'He may have been poisoned. Or he may have committed suicide', answered my companion

'What do you mean?'

'Well, your husband.'

'Pardon, sir, but I'm his sister,' she interrupted

'Pardon me. Anyhow, he was found dead in Mr Charles' Flat with no evidence showing a third person was among them,' continued my companion.

'Did you happen to notice what he was carrying in his bag before he took off from here?' I asked

'No, unfortunately, I was asleep at the time, but he usually takes a bottle of wine with him to breakfast with Mr Charles, an old friend of his', she answered.

'Do you know what wine your brother will take with him beforehand?'

'No, he usually chooses one randomly from his collection. That's what he told me.'

'Are you able to tell how many bottles are missing from his collection?'

'I can't really tell. I did not concern myself with my brother's collection and did not give it a thought before. What if any of the maids could've known what bottle he would take?'

'I don't think so. My brother was not the companionable type. He would stay in his room after coming from work.'

'I see.'

'I would like to inform you that we only have one maid and a cook.'

'Why is that?' asked my companion.

'We, my brother, and I, usually clean around behind us and we passably don't need many maids.'

'Do you know anyone who might want to poison your brother?' I asked.

'No. My brother was a good man. I can't think of anybody wanting to murder him.'

'Did anyone possess any type of hatred towards your brother?' asked my companion.

'No. Like I said, he was a good man.'

'Maybe someone from work. Can't you think of anyone who might have poisoned your brother and gained something from his death?' persisted my friend.

'No, I can-…come to think of it. His trading partner, Mr Terry H-, came some days a week ago and argued with my brother. I did not hear what the argument was about, but I heard words like, "You can't" and "It's absurd".'

'Do you know anyone else who might be suspicious?'

'…No, I can't think of anybody else.'

'That's okay mademoiselle. Can we speak with the maids?'

'Oh, there is only one maid and a cook if you wish to speak to them.'

'Yes, if you may', said I as she rose from her seat and went to inform the maid and the cook. Looking closely at the sitting-room, it was crowded with wine bottles. Not just that, the English wine was ordered in an alphabetical order showing his immense care and his organized manners. He also had wine from all over the world. I saw Italian, Japanese, French, and many other labels on the wine bottles. He was passionate about wine that is what I infer studying his compendium.

'A strong woman, isn't she?' exclaimed my friend.

'Indeed, she is. How she managed to hold her tears and speak naturally though all the queries.'

'But who knows, she might be the killer hiding behind the captivating mask aping to be the heart-broken sister' exclaimed my companion

'If so, then she is performing splendidly', I replied. Moments later, the maid and the cook came to the sitting-room. The maid looked dejected, but the cook was acting as if nothing happened.

'Do you know anyone who possessed hatred towards your master?' asked Mr Vandican. Both started speaking, but the cook paused and let the maid continue.

'No, I don't know anything about Mr Robert's affairs.'

'Same', continued the cook.

'Wait! Remember… Yesterday, Mr Terry came and had a quarrel with Mr Robert. You remember, right?' asked the cook after a few moments.

'Oh, yes, I remember now. What is that? If I heard what they were talking about? No, unfortunately, I did not, but their voices were somewhat in a high tone.'

'I assume Mr Robert chooses a wine bottle randomly from the collection. Is that correct?' I asked

'Yes, that is true.' Answered the cook and they both agreed upon the fact.

'Do you think you can tell how many bottles he took with him today'?

'I don't think so. He is the one that usually cleans his collection. He doesn't like anyone to touch it', answered the maid.

'I seldom come to the sitting-room; thus, I can't really tell', answered the cook.

'Fair enough. If you may, please call Ms Anderson', I asked.

'Surely, sir'

'Yes? Can I help you, furthermore, sirs?' asked the appealing lady.

'Do you happen to know where Mr Terry lives?'

'No, regrettably I don't know, but he lives here in West-moor that's all I can help you with, I'm sorry' she replied.

'Alas, we will have to ask through the households again my friend' I exclaimed with disappointment

'We will be going now, mademoiselle.' As we were going out, she said with waterworks in her eyes, 'Please find the person who murdered my brother.'

'Don't worry my lady. I'm confident we will find him.'

'I would owe you my life, sir.'

'Oh, don't me…', as I was talking, my companion interrupted and told Ms Anderson, 'Can you inform inspector Gerard, who will be coming here soon, that we are at Mr Terry's household if you may?'

'Bu-but aren't you detectives.' I did not see her face for we did not answer her query and were walking out of the household, but I'm quite certain it was a bewildered face.

'A remarkable case', said I, as we were walking to a random household asking for directions to Mr Terry's household.

'Yes, it is a peculiar case' replied my companion with a face that told me that he needs to reflect. As no other words were spoken between us, the time passed quite sluggishly until we lastly found Mr Terry's household.

EPISODE IX:
WHAT TERRY
H- HAD TO SAY

Just as Mr Anderson's house, Mr Terry's house was rather of the same massiveness, which suggested that their business was quite profitable.

'How can I help you, sirs?' was the query asked by the bright-blond haired, chiseled jaw lined, and smooth-skinned mademoiselle opening the door for our ringing of the doorbell. 'Is Mr Terry at home you ask? Y-yes, he is in his study... Can you come in? Moments sirs, will ask my husband. Understood, will inform him that you are detectives that are here to ask him a few queries.' After a couple of minutes, she came back, gesturing for us to come in, while helping us with our coats and hats.

'Please wait in the sitting-room, Mr Terry will arrive soon.' Not a minute passed since the lady left and we could hear footsteps rushing downstairs and suddenly an individual enters the room.

'What happened? With what can I help you?' Neither of us replied but just stared at the figure that we assumed to be Mr Terry, bending his back and placing his hands on his knees while exhaling and inhaling air.

'You should do some movement sometimes sir, or I believe your health will become worse than it is now if you keep it this way', I remarked without giving notice to Mr Terry's queries. 'Take a seat and relax, and then we can continue our discussion.'

After Mr Terry regained his natural state Mr Vandican and I recalled the details of the murder to him and as anybody would react, Mr Terry reacted broken heartedly and showed the sorrowfulness upon knowing this news.

'Now, we would like to ask you some queries.' Said I.

'Absolutely, sir. Pray, proceed with your queries— Last time I saw Mr Robert? I saw him some days ago. I went up to his house and discussed a business matter. What? You heard that I argued with him? Well, to be honest, we were arguing a bit. Each one with his outlook, so I think it is something typical to argue. What was the argument about? Mr Anderson wanted to retire from trading and follow his passion for writing stories or something. Obviously, I was opposed to this and told him about my view on the matter and that he should continue. How did the matter end? Well, it didn't. I told him that I would leave him a couple of days to reconsider his judgment. Yes, I knew that every Saturday he would go to Mr Charles' Place. I did go there a couple of times with him. Depressing business that they both had to decease. If he had enemies? I don't think so. I just know that he did not have a snug relationship with his sister. He always came here complaining about her. What was the reason for the hateful relationship? I don't really know. When I say complained I mean that he complained about how inconsiderate and uncaring she is. He didn't specify what happened. When was the last time I saw—' while completing his response, the bright-blonde haired, chiseled jaw lined, and smooth-skinned mademoiselle entered the sitting-room?

'Not now, Cecil. I'm busy', cried Mr Terry.

'What's wrong? why are these gentlemen here to ask you questions?' she asked uncertainly. There was no reply by Mr Terry, so I had to break the silence, 'Your husband's friend, Mr Robert Anderson, died today, so we are here to ask some queries.'

'What! Oh no! How could thi…' Saying these words, she paused suddenly. Her reaction was somewhat peculiar in way. I can't say why, but I had the intuition that something was wrong.

'You seem to have known him. When was the last time you saw him?' asked my companion.

'Last time I saw him…las-last week, when he was here for dinner', she answered unsurely. I couldn't continue to be asking queries for I noticed some drops of tears sliding through her cheeks. I paused for a moment observing her, and something hit me.

'Mrs. Cecil, what a coruscating ring you're wearing. May I study it? I am fond of these things', I asked excitingly.

'Surely', she answered. I took the ring and observed it closely and gave it back to her.

'For how long have you been married?' I asked.

'9 years', answered the tearful lady after some moments while her husband was still thinking of the answer.

'What does this have to do with the death of my friend?' asked the husband, furiously.

'Oh nothing, just wondering', I replied. 'Mr Vandican, do want to add any more queries?'

'Just one more, I can't observe anyone else in the house with the anomaly for both of you. I presume that you neither have maids, butlers, nor cooks?'

'Indeed, you are correct. We are the only two living in the house. It might be weird, living in a house like this with no help, but it is something that runs in the family. We just bring a housecleaner two times per week to help me clean', replied the lady.

'I understand now, cheers'

'Well then, if that's all, let us return to Ms Anderson's household. We need to ask her various queries.'

When I initially entered the sitting-room, I smelled a rosy scent. The same type of fragrance at Mr Charles' floristry.' I looked attentively through the room and saw a cosmic bouquet of Mister Lincoln's roses. I simultaneously asked, 'These roses, where were they purchased from?' There was silence for some jiffies when the wife answered, 'My husband purchased them for me yesterday.'

'Where were they purchased from?' I asked eagerly.

'I don't know. A young man came yesterday with this bouquet and said that it's from Mr Terry.'

'Really…' I turned my gaze to Mr Terry, 'From where did you purchase them?'

'From Mr Charles. As I stated, he was my friend as well.' As I was going to reply, Mr Vandican intervened, looking at me and saying, 'I reason we shall go now, correct?'

'Indeed, but before I go. Mr Terry, did you murder Mr Charles and Mr Robert?' I felt the changing of the aurora in the room upon my asking this query but anyhow I kept observing Mr Terry.

'By George! what are you saying!? I didn't murder anyone, and in accumulation, I would not gain anything from his death', he cried furiously while gazing at me, then changing his gaze to my companion for a split second and returning it to me.

'I suppose it's true, anyway au revoir, let us go Mr Vandican.'

EPISODE X:

THE TURN OF THE TABLES

'**W**hat was all that about?' Asked Mr Vandican while walking down the paths towards Ms Anderson's house.

'Nothing, just a random query. Nothing more, nothing less.' I replied. 'Did you notice anything peculiar?' He looked at me upon my asking this query.

'Not really. Did you?' He asked.

'Yes, I think so.'

'And what is it?'

'The ring', I answered. He was still gazing at me, but his expression changed to a confused one.

'What about it?'

'Well it was scratched, and her ring finger was of the same colour as the others.' My companion was still looking bewildered.

'I don't get the point. Care to explain?'

'Everything will be clarified at a certain moment', I answered, and until we arrived at the house, there was no discussion between us.

We arrived at the house, and from the looks of things, inspector Gerard had arrived. We entered the house explaining who we are and entered the sitting-room where everyone was.

'Inspector! Good to see you again. Seems like you are doing a delightful job so far', exclaimed my friend.

'I'm doing quite well, what about yourselves. Find anything?'

'Well yes, if you may come with us to another room so we can discuss', said I. Latter we briefly explained to the prefect what we have observed and deduced.

'Another thing inspector, was there cyanide in the sealed wine bottle?' I asked eagerly after we have finished our narration.

'No, there was none. The cyanide was in the opened wine on the table', he answered.

'Interesting, cheers', I replied

We returned to the sitting-room, where the sister of the deceased was. We had informed the prefect that we would like to ask her some queries about her relationship with her brother, which he approved.

'Ms Anderson, we have heard that your relationship with your brother was rather an unhappy one. Why so?' I asked while my sub-conscious was admiring her beauty.

'It looks like they have told you. Very well. Our relationship was not a happy one. Robert only cared about himself. He would come from work and close himself in his room until the next morning. I wanted to get closer to him, but he always repelled me. He began getting colder and colder when the only time I could see him was when he was returning from work. I did not know if he hated me, so I always brought up this subject, every time I could, in front of him. That is it!' At the moment, we didn't know if she was telling the truth or not, but from a physiological perspective, if she was lying, then she was a first-rate liar.

'Now that he is dead, who inherits him?' Asked Mr Vandican without prior notice.

'Where are you getting at? You don't think that—'

'Yes, I think that you may have murdered him for inheriting his fortune. After all, he was a wealthy man. Now remember, lying is no good. If you required money so badly that you would have to murder him, we will eventually know', declared my companion. She paused for a moment, thought about his remark and said, 'Robert was an inconsiderately conceited man. I required money badly, but he refused to help me. I had nowhere I could work. Still, he refused to help me. I brought this matter up to him plenty of times, but I was talking to a wall. Now that he's finally dead, I can inherit him.'

There was a long pause when she finished her narrative in which all of us gazed at her with no words that could respond to what she said.

'Well if you're the killer, you're rather bold for your remark', said the prefect.'

'I agree, but did you murder him?' She turned her gaze towards me and answered with bold the statement, 'I did

55

not kill my brother', while turning her gaze towards the prefect.

'Okay then, I think we sought what we were looking for. If you may excuse us', Said I. we rose from our seats and were about to leave the house when I asked Mr Vandican to wait for me outside, for I required the bathroom. He acted upon my request and went outside, closing the door behind him. Upon my return from the bathroom, I reentered the sitting-room to ask Ms Anderson a query.

'Excuse me mademoiselle, but I still have a query in my mind. Do you think your brother was having a relationship with a woman? Or maybe an affair?' She looked at me for a few moments. Bewildered by the query that was irrelevant to his murder, but she answered lastly, 'Come to think of it, once a month he would sleep outside the house, saying that he was busy and couldn't return. Of course, I believed him, but there were some queries behind those actions. Maybe it was an affair.'

'Do you happen to know where he stayed for those couple of days? A hotel? Something?'

'Yes, he informed me that he stays at a friend's house, but it was odd for when he came back, his boots were always polished.'

'Excuse the query.' I interrupted 'But why is it… Oh yes… I see now, thank you, mademoiselle.'

I went outside, and it was about 30 minutes to 5. We still had 30 minutes to catch the train returning to London. While going to the train station I declared 'Mr Vandican, from now, I would like each one of us to investigate this case individually to see who arrives at the murderer first.' He looked at me and replied 'A fine proposal. Agreed!'

EPISODE XI:

MEDITATION

We arrived at 221b Baker Street, and I went promptly to my study. The case was a simple one from my bird's-eye view. It was a symphony case. Or as Mr Holmes would call it "An x pipe case". I sat on the settee and started listening to Beethoven's 5th symphony, recalling the events and details of the day, from the beginning, till the end. Doing that, I will optimistically distinguish the murderer. I listened to the music, and my mind started running its train of thoughts instantaneously.

EPISODE XII:
MR HOLMES'
METHOD:
RATIOCINATION &
TRAIN OF CONCEPT

Part one of the investigation: Two victims were poisoned in a flat. There wasn't a poison bottle in the flat of Mr Charles' Nor Mr Robert's which suggested that it wasn't double-suicide nor homicide-suicide. Cyanide was planted in the wine bottle thence; the poison came from outside by either one of the deceased. If I know the source of the wine, I catch the murderer.

Mr Charles owns a floristry and is a poor fellow with no relatives. Mr Robert was a wine trader and lives in Westmoor. He is a wealthy man and had recently decided to retire and be a writer. We were highly inclined to think that the murderer came from Mr Robert's side.

Part two of the investigation: Involved us going to the households of the deceased. We did not go to any of Mr Charles' Relatives for he did not have any.

Ms Anderson was the first one we interrogated. She knew about her brother's habit of leaving every Saturday to go to Mr Charles. She says she does not know what wine bottle he would take with him, and the reason is that he takes one from his collection unsystematically. Thence, she would not know which bottle to plant the poison in.

She has a deep hatred for her brother and will inherit his wealth now that he passed away. She also advised us that Mr Robert has a business partner whom he works with and that he had argued with him recently. When asked if she may be the murderer, she acted boldly, and her eyes contacted mine which suggested that if she is indeed the killer, we are dealing with a cold-hearted manipulative type.

Mr Terry was the second one interrogated. He also knew about Mr Terry's habit. He claims that he had quarrelled with Mr Robert for Mr Robert wanted to retire from trading while Mr Terry did not want that to ensue. Mrs Cecil entered the sitting-room at that time and was devastated by the news of Mr Robert's death. That was an eccentrical thing I supposed for he is just a friend of her husband's… Or is he not?

I claimed that I wanted to observe her ring when I wanted to observe something else. It was just as I expected. The ring was scratched, and her ring finger's colour was of the same colour as the others and did not bare the ring's mark. I remembered that I asked Mrs Anderson if her brother was having a relationship and she replied with a, "Possibly", and the reason for that is that when he came from work, his boots where polished. She supposed that if he had indeed stayed in his friend's household, his boots would have been grimy looking, exactly as he left with them. Nowadays, some hotels take their costumers' Boots and polish them. That was what made her reason that he was having a relationship or an affair. Certainly, that does not mean that he may be having an affair but merging this fact together with Mrs Terry's ring and her reaction suggested that he was having an affair with her. My father always used to tell me *"A woman has two mouths that she uses to speak. From one, the lie, and from the other, the truth"*. I suppose his words came in handy today.

I may need to make inquiries tomorrow about the velvet flowers, found at Mr Terry's house today. I may also need to confirm the affair by making some inquiries for the hotels that polish their costumers' Boots for these two points grasp the key to our mystery. Mr Terry, when asked if he is the murderer, stumbled for a second and reacted in a peculiar way. If I remember correctly, he stared at me then turned his gaze to Mr Vandican for a split second, then retu… Oh… This cannot be. Now that I examine our interview with Mr Terry psychologically… this case is indeed solemn. It is grotesque. I must act immediately!

For my esteemed readers, who did not understand what I had acquired, you may know the truth at the end of the story, or you can find it out yourself by returning to the interview and examining it yourselves.

EPISODE XIII:
THE FORETELLING
OF A SCHEME

'**M**r Vandican! Can I have some of your time?' I asked as I raised my voice for him to perceive. I heard his footsteps. Thus, I went back to the study and waited for him to come in.

'Yes, what is it?'

'I've finished recalling my case, and I know who the murderer is. Did you?'

'I did indeed find out.'

'That is good, let's hear your explanation first.'

'As you wish.' Said he as he prepared himself to narrate his induction by closing his eyes and remembering some of the details. 'First of all, I would like to say that I took this case the old-fashioned way and I asked myself. Who gained from the death of both men? The only person that came to my mind was Ms Anderson. Indeed, she may have said that Mr Robert took a wine bottle randomly, and she would not know which bottle to place the poison in, but it may be a lie altogether. What proves her statement that she does not know what wine he would take? She is also the one capable of putting cyanide inside his wine and then throwing the cyanide bottle away. She looked-for money and her brother did not want to give her any. Hence, the only resolution was to inherit him. She may have acted boldly, but she is a strong woman remember. She may have acted this way to throw off suspicions surrounding her. Who would say, in front of the prefect, that he or she would gain from someone's death and state a crucial matter so boldly? People would say that it is because he or she is not the killer they are acting this way, but no, I reason she acted this way to throw off suspicions around her. And if you think about it, you may think so too. I still fail to find evidence, but I think we may find something soon.'

'Remarkable! The way your mind works is so pure, my friend.'

'Well if it catches the killer why complicate things?', he said with a beam that contained a puff of confidence. 'What's your theory then? I said mine. Your turn.'

'Indeed. Let me start off, mon amie, by saying that Mr Robert Anderson was having an affair with Mrs Cecil.'

'What! In God's name, Mr Joy. How did you come up with such an idea?' exclaimed Mr Vandican with confusion.

'Let me finish my dear friend. If you will remember, her reaction to Mr Robert's death was somehow not that of a friend but much more than that. She was devastated when she heard about his death. Always remember that a woman speaks at the same time. From her mouth and from her eyes. Adjoin that to the fact that her ring was scratched, and her ring finger was not tanned. A woman's most precious jewellery is her marriage ring. Why would Mrs Cecil act in a such a reckless manner towards the ring and attire it seldom? Let us ask this query from another perspective. When would you take off your marriage ring and act recklessly towards it?'

'Perhaps… When I take a bath', answered my companion. 'That's a possibility, yes, but it does not explain why her skin isn't tanned, and the ring is scratched.'

'What do you suggest then?' asked Mr Vandican

'If I am married and I am having an affair, will you meet your secret lover with your marriage ring on?'

'Oh…The answer is simple if you place it this way. But if she was having an affair with him, why kill him?'

'"*Don't theorise without enough evidence*"', mentioned Mr Holmes once to Dr Watson. Anyhow, let me carry on.'

'Pray, do so.'

'We know now that an affair had been happening. Whom would act furiously knowing this affair is occurring? Yes, the person in your mind, but not just that. My intuition tells me that he had an accomplice. He is too incompetent and dim-witted. He cannot come up with a plan like this. There must have been an accomplice.' Mr Vandican looked at me eagerly and asked, 'And whom do you think is this accomplice?'

'I still don't know, but my suspicions surround Ms Anderson for both would gain something from his death, one financially and one revengefully.' 'I get your point now. I think I am convinced with your theory, but do you have the last link?' Asked my companion excitingly.

'I have a 50% chance of getting the last link with a scheme I have in my mind. We would know for surly tomorrow morning for Mr Terry will fall in my webs.'

'In all aspects, I suspect that tomorrow will be that last of our little escapade and we will know for sure whom this accomplice is', said I with the air of aristocracy. Mr Vandican was lost in his thoughts for some moments, but he broke the silence eventually, 'Regrettably, sir, tomorrow is my fishing day. I can't accompany you with the scheme, but nevertheless, I would appreciate your own account of how the adventure ended tomorrow evening.'

'That is a letdown, but it would be my honour to narrate the adventure tomorrow evening!'

EPISODE XIV:
THE WESTMOOR
MYSTERY

I woke up the next morning, and the first thing upon my mind was to ask all the hotels that polish their costumers' Boots in London about Mr Robert and Mrs Cecil. I did my research and founded that there is a total of 6 hotels that polish their costumers' Boots. Upon knowing the names of these hotels, I went straight to each one of them with the same query, 'Did a man by the name of Robert Anderson come in here once every month or a couple of months?, 'Did a woman by the name of Cecil take up a room once every month or couple of months?', and 'Does a couple take up a room every once a month or couple of months?' In which all the hotels replied with the same answer 'You mean the famously known wine trader? Unfortunately, he did not take any room here; it would have been a wonderful thing for the hotel if he would've come.'

Upon their answers, I distinguished that the deceased was using a fake name. Same goes with Mrs Cecil. I also believe that they did not arrive at the hotel together at once. I quite believe they arrived separately as an additional precaution. These were the results of my first task, and woefully, nothing was gained from my early survey. I hence, knew that the whole case bore upon the second task which was to call upon the prefect and Stevie to come by my flat and ask Stevie a couple of queries for, theoretically, he is the second task.

At, roughly speaking, a quarter past eleven, both of them were in my study. I told the prefect about my view and induction of this mystery, with the anomaly of the part with an accomplice, in which he partially accepts until we find the last link.

'Stevie, the whole case depends upon you now', I remarked.

'Ye-yes sir.'

'Well, then. When you delivered the flower bouquet to Westmoor, more precisely to Mr Terry's household, the other day, did they pay for the bouquet you had delivered?'

'No sir, Mr Charles told me that someone would come by at the floristry and pay for it', answered the lad immediately.

'Good. When you came back from your adventure did you happen to notice a bag near Mr Charles or a bag that Mr Charles wouldn't usually have?' I asked the query while every nerve in my body bore with exhilaration for the answer.

'Well... Hum... atter of fact, there was one. When we were closing the floristry, he was carrying a bag with him that I was not familiar with. I didn't pay much attention to it back then.'

'This settles it. Inspector, in that bag, was the poisoned wine. And I am sure we will find the fingerprints of the bag to match those of Mr Terry. We must, without delay, leave for Westmoor and take him into custody before he vanishes from the surface of the earth.'

'What makes you so sure that inside the bag was the poisoned wine? And what makes you think that Mr Terry went to Mr Charles the other day to pay? Why wasn't Mrs Cecil?' Asked the prefect.

'Mr Robert always brought one wine bottle with him, and it was the one sealed on the table. The only other person that could've have brought the wine was Mr Charles. Mr Terry mentioned that he went to Mr Charles occasionally. Suppose Mr Terry would go to Mr Charles and give him a wine bottle telling him that it is a gift from him. Everything fits into place. Also, Mrs Cecil was the one who opened the door for Stevie. She couldn't be in London and Westmoor at the same time unless she is indeed a celestial being.'

'I see now. Well then, I think we have time to catch the 12 p.m. train to Westmoor.'

Half an hour later we were on the train heading to Westmoor. Upon our arrival there, we at once went to Mr Terry's household. We rang the bell, but there was no answer. We knocked on the door, and there was no answer either. I asked the prefect to take the precaution of breaking the door for we mustn't lose time for he may have gotten away by now. Approving my request, we burst the door open and entered the house!

The aurora that filled the house was of complete silence and grotesquery. 'Mr Terry' and 'Mrs. Cecil' were the names we cried out as we were moving from one room to another, searching for them until the moment, we saw the bathroom door open and peeked inside. At that instant, we realised that the devil himself had rejuvenated. It was no work of a human being, to put it this way.

Entering the bathroom—I must say that I would do my best to describe the scene as mild as possible for it was the most wicked and macabre sight I have seen in my life—Mr Terry's head was gashed off. Not merely that, but his entire body was gashed into pieces and thrown into the bath sink. Who would have the heart to do such a flagitious thing?

We were standing at the door of the bathroom for more than 1 minute. Just standing tranquil, processing what had happened in this house in the past 24 hours.

We regained our consciousness of reality and searched the whole house for Mrs Cecil but with no seeds. We returned, at that point, to the bathroom and using Mr Holmes' Methodology, I began to study the crime scene. The first thing I noticed was that it was too much blood in the bath sink for one person only. That was a point kept in my mind.

I studied the floor, but it was clean, save only some drops of blood, but when I looked closely, I remarked 'Halloo! … What is this!' A drip of blood stepped on by a boot. That bore a crucial clue to the mystery.

There were no other clues in the bathroom, so I widened the field outside. Going out of the bathroom, I was in the sitting-room which I investigated. There was nothing that bore the signs of struggle, but when I looked at the carpet of the sitting-room I saw tenuous signs of something being dragged to the bathroom. Hence, the place of the crime was not in the bathroom, but, maybe,

Mr Terry was knocked out with something heavy on his head that made him unconscious. I examined the corpse head upon this idea, but there was no sign of it being hit, but then, when I was examining the head, I saw a bizarre materialistic clue in the bath sink. I bent down and approached my hand to seize it, but the inspector was earlier.

'What is this!? I think, Mr Joy, that this case is settled.' The object being seized by the inspector was Mrs Cecil's ring.

'With this evidence, I think the mystery ought to be solved, but tell me, what do you make of this case?' I asked

'Well, it's obvious, isn't it? As you had mentioned, an affair was occurring between Mr Robert and Mr Terry's wife. Devastated was the wife that she suspected her husband for Mr Robert's death. Taking reprisal afterwards, in a rather more grotesque manner than usual, and flying away as fast as she could, for she did not take any luggage with her, realising this fact after searching through her closet. Evidently, after killing her husband and before leaving, she threw her marriage ring into the bath sink. She must be a fool for doing such a thing', answered the inspector confidently.

'Inspector', said I, 'I'm dejected in saying this, but, if Mr Holmes was to be solving this case with us, he would have been, unquestionably, downhearted upon us.'

'Why would you say so?' asked the prefect, crossly.

'For we have, unfortunately, committed some gaffes which he had forewarned us about umpteen times', I answered.

'And what may those gaffes be?' Asked the prefect sardonically.

'Well', I answered, 'For your case, I expect him to crit-icise you by saying *"It is a capital mistake to theorise before one has data."* While for my case he would undeniably say, *"The more outré and grotesque an incident is the more carefully it deserves to be examined"*. Nevertheless, if the case is how you say it is, then you would find Mrs Cecil the murderer with ease for she couldn't have gone far from here as she is a recognizable woman. In any case. I want you to tell the press that the crime occurred in the bathroom with the victim being murdered in it, and don't want you to include any other part of the house.' I discussed the case with the prefect for a petite while afterwards and then returned to London.

I returned to 221b Baker Street by evening, and Mr Vandican was anticipating my arrival to congratulate me of my part in solving the crime.

'How did you…', I asked pausing in the middle, think-ing of how the news got to him.

'The evening papers. All the details are in the papers, sir. Although it is too bad that another criminal is walk-ing the streets, I'm sure the yard will locate Mrs Cecil in no time for she had acted out of grief. I do not think she is in her full cerebral health. In any case, you did a respectable job', vaunted my companion.

'I did nothing, just method and ratiocination. Anyhow, it has been a busy 48 hours. I will, probably, vegetate for some days.' I declared while mounting the stairs to Mr Holmes' bedroom or, somehow, my bedroom currently.

EPISODE XV:
THE EXPOS
OF THE
SCHEME

A couple of days have passed, and you are, my esteemed readers, in the present where you have started. Currently, all of England was searching for Mrs Cecil. Any person walking the streets alone would fear for his life thinking a fanatic murderer is walking freely on the streets. It seemed that the papers altered the news from the death of Mr Charles and Mr Robert to the search of a fanatic murderer. Ironically, my name was slightly mentioned in the papers. I greatly expect my name to wonder through civilians. In any case, we are back in 221b Baker Street, where I was asking my companion to recall some events that I fail to remember.

'Can you remind me of some of the details about Mr Terry's case, which I fail to remember, and I highly need it for finalizing my escapade?' I asked while looking at him as he turned around and sat back on his seat.

'With pleasure. What do you need to know?'

'Mr Terry was married to his wife for nine years, correct?'

'Yes, if I remember correctly.'

'Hum…Mr Terry's cadaver was found in the bathroom sink, but the experts suggested that he was initially murdered in the bathroom. That was true, isn't it?'

'Let's see. If I remember correctly. They said that he was murdered in the bathroom.'

'It seems that I remember now. A moment to write these facts on a note… One last thing, what was the weapon used to murder Mr Terry?'

'I believe a kitchen knife', he answered, thinking a few moments before doing so.

'You have a good memory I perceive, a moment to write this note…That would do, cheers my friend.'

'It's nothing. Anything else?'

'Yes, one last thing my friend… Please, avow your crimes of murdering Mr Terry and being his accomplice for murdering Mr Charles and Mr Robert.'

EPISODE XVI:

A CHESS GAME

If a natural disaster is occurring at this moment, then neither of us is paying attention to it for the intensity of the moment speaks for itself.

'H-huh what do you mean?' asked Mr Vandican, breaking the silence.

'You will act like every other criminal before he confesses his crime. Very well, I will prove it to you now.'

'If this is a kind of joke then it's a cynical one, my friend. You know that Mrs Cecil is on the run. She is the murderer; you have said it yourself', said my friend getting up from his seat.

'Joke? Oh, no-no. You know perfectly well what I am talking about. Mrs Cecil is just a part of the whole mystery, my friend', I replied, holding his elbow as if to say, "Back to your seat".

'I assure you it's not funny.'

'You can be your natural self after you hear what I have to say, and I would like to hear your motive for these crimes for I can't think of any reasonable one.'

'What motive are you talking about Mr Joy!? Do you have a fever?' He asked, but I continued my narrative either way.

'Mr Charles and Mr Robert were killed by a person who was acquainted with the fact that every Saturday, they would meet up bringing a wine bottle. You were one of the people who knew that, but at that time I didn't suspect you.'

'Realizing that Mr Charles has no relatives, the only other suspects are Mr Robert's sister, trading partner, and the landlord. I will exclude the landlord for there was no evidence indicating he went to Westmoor and since he will gain nothing from their death. Thus, let us move to the other two suspects. Ms Anderson was a suspect until we went to Mr Terry's house.'

'If you are the one who thought of the plan, then, Mr Terry had deliberately flunked it. Upon our arrival, he acted in an outré manner. You did also act strangely. In our interview there, he seldom looked at you, and you seldom asked queries. Something was out of its place. You did not know each other, so why? I asked myself.'

'At first, I did not give it a thought, but when I recalled the events later that day, I remembered that when he was asked if he is the murderer, he gazed at me then turned his gaze towards you for a split second and returned it to me. If one looks at this incident from a perspective of a typical person, one would say that nothing is out of the ordinary, but when one looks at the incident from a psychologist's perspective, one would most certainly say that that was not the first time Mr Terry is meeting you. It was strange enough that you knew him, and you did not tell me about it. Why? It will evidently cause fingers to point at you.'

'Another thing that occurred is that when I commenced asking about the flowers, you instinctively changed the subject. That was the second suspicion.'

'After we arrived that day to London from Westmoor, I knew that three things were facts: [1] Mr Terry ordered flowers from Mr Charles' Floristry the day before the murder [2] Mr Robert was having an affair with Mr Terry's wife [3] If Mr Terry was the murderer, then he had an accomplice, for he is too incompetent and dim-witted for such things.'

'Running the events through my mind, I came to a fourth fact, and that's that Mr Terry knew you. I, upon distinguishing these facts, set my hypothesis into play, and I suggested to you that Mr Terry had an accomplice. I then suggested that we would know this accomplice after we interrogate Mr Terry.'

'My approach was to root a fear of betrayal towards your accomplice. You would act, realising that there is a chance of betrayal, impulsively by murdering your accomplice and blaming it on the x accomplice that I suggested initially. I had to try this through, or I had no evidence to accuse Mr Terry when I knew, for a fact, that he was the murderer. I cared less for the death of a murderer who murdered an impeccant man, Mr Charles, for personal vengeance.'

'What I expected was that you would craft evidence to blame Ms Anderson for the murder, but I did not envisage you to have this idea of making the wife appear as the maniac murderer on the run. It was an ingenious move, I acknowledge that. It may have slipped the yard but not me, my friend. You're in checkmate', said I with a gentle beam

'But his wife is on the run! The yard stated that she's on the run!' interrupted my companion, contradicting me.

'My friend, you always have the habit of interrupting me. Let me finish', I replied to his words, while watching him sitting down calmly. 'Why would somebody murder a person in such a way? I have put myself in the murderer's place just as Mr Holmes once said, and it hit me. There was a lot of blood in the crime scene. At first, it seemed normal. Any inspector would say it's the victim's blood, something ordinary. It was an ingenious move I admit now that I think about it. You came up with the idea to kill Mr Terry and his wife and make it appear that she had killed him, for killing her secret lover and flew away. But what had happed was that you had murdered them both. You had to find a way to take Mrs Cecil's body out of the house with you, but it seemed an impossible task for it will be, obviously, noticed. You came up, at that point, with the notion of cutting her body into pieces and putting them in a container or something of that sort. Upon this notion, you had acted and had taken the body out with you, on your self-proclaimed "fishing day", as fishing tools in a container that you would throw away in the water later that day. Obviously, upon slashing Mr Cecil, you came upon the problem that you would have to gash Mr Terry's body as well to conceal any evidence referring to Mrs Cecil slaughter. Upon this notion, I took samples of the blood from the bath sink and asked experts to check if it is the same type of blood. To my relief, it wasn't.'

'My suspicions were complete. You are the accomplice and the slaughterer. Distinguishing that, I wanted to deliberately hoodwink you and take you into my confidence so what I did was: [1] I told the prefect my induction and the evidence of the blood— By this I mean that he knows everything about my case's wires— [2] I ordered the prefect to search all the areas in and near London and Westmoor for Mrs Cecil's cadaver confidentially, without anyone comprehending. [3] I told him only to mention that Mr Terry's cadaver was found in the bathroom and that his wife had murdered him for killing her lover without anything else to be said.'

'The results of this was that we found the remains of Mrs Cecil in a fishing area near Westmoor. Why did I suggest a fishing area you may ask yourself? That is because you had informed me the day before the slaughter that you were going fishing the day of the murder. Matter of fact, where is a more suitable place to hide a cadaver than beneath the water?... Do you care to confess now?'

'Unfortunately, it's all a theory' He implied.

'Unfortunately for you mon amie, that theory has evidence.'

'Care to lay them?' contradicted my companion.

'Very well, no one knew where the body was initially murdered with the anomaly of certain people only. I must say you were not fooled by this part, but you were by the other. No one mentioned that the body was gashed with a kitchen knife. It wasn't mentioned in the papers. How come you know about this fact when you weren't even present at the crime scene?'

'I believe most crimes happen with a kitchen knife. It was an instinct; nothing more nothing less. And if I happened to slaughter them, how come no one noticed me? I am sure that if they were slaughtered in such a fashion, there would be blood all over my clothes. How do you explain that?' interrupted my companion.

'You say an intuition from God… I state that the yard had also found garments covered with blood, under the water, where Mrs Cecil's body was found, wrapped with heavy gravels so that it bowls.'

'It does not bear any evidence towards me. Anyone could have done it.'

'Anyone could have done it, indeed, but in this case, no one could have done it except you, Mr Vandican!'

'Where is your evidence that you fail to lay upon the table?'

'Fair enough, I only desired your own good, but it's too late. The evidence that you have not noticed yet and must tolerate in mind is that when you were busy slaughtering Mrs Cecil and her husband, you stepped on a drop of blood with your boots. I am sure if we examine your boots, you will appear guilty. It is absolute that you're the murderer. My friend, there is no way out of this. If only you would conf—....'

EPISODE XVII:
THE
DECLARATION
OF CULPABILITY

'Indeed, I murdered Terry and his wife and was the mastermind behind the plan of murdering Charles and Robert. I am the one who gave the poisoned wine bottle to Terry H- and instructed him to give it to Charles outside his Flat. How dim-witted can you be to order flowers to your own house? Upon seeing those flowers, I wanted to conceal their importance, but unfortunately, you noticed them. I realised at that point that Terry would be apprehended eventually. So, I had to make him silent. The rest was just as you said. It's as if you were present at the moment of the crime.'

'Anyhow, you want a resolution for doing this devilish act? Fair enough, the reason I'm about to lay before you, will only be comprehended by the ones who have been through it.'

'My reason goes back to when I was a fella in Australia. I lived in poverty for my father was unable to find a persistent job for he was an alcoholic. Subsequently, my mother deserted us for she could not stand the state we were in. I was left with an alcoholic father who, however, did not desert my side and took charge of me. We struggled settling in a place and had to change households frequently. These events happened when I was 15 years of age. Things did not seem to get better pending one day, my father received a telegraph. I was present at the moment he opened the telegraph, and upon reading it, a smile took the shape of his face. I've never thought that I would see a smile on my father's face again. He commenced reading the telegraph, and upon concluding it, he threw it on the table and commenced giving out a laugh that displayed his vast contentment. I inquired if I could see what the message is about, and he handed it to me with pleasure. If I remember the message's words properly, I quite believe it ran as so':

"Dear Vandican,

I was probing for your whereabouts for some stint, and I have, ultimately, reached it. I have heard about your sombre state, and I could not vacate a valued friend in such a state. I have informed the Professor about you in which he has orchestrated your return to England this week. I demand your proficient dexterities in London. Professor Moriarty asks for your aid. I hope you accept his proposal.

Best regards, Steven Stern"'

'Upon reading the message, I asked my father the obvious query "who is this vague man that hands us his aid?" in which his response was as forthright as a child's "An old fellow. A fellow that I have been anticipating his message for such a long time. Prepare yourself. We are going to London. My friends need my aid, and they shall have it."

'In less than a week, we had already settled in a house in London. It seemed like a chimera. I had already forgotten that we were living in poverty back in Australia. I constantly speculated who this x man might be. Even my father's manners changed upon our arrival. It seemed that he had left alcoholism. It was a delightful reverie, but not for so long. Some years had passed, and in just one day, everything changed. I returned from school that day to find out that my father had committed suicide. I was demolished. I had no relatives in London with the anomaly of my father. My only family had left me in the vilest way. "Why would he commit suicide?" That query did not reside in my mind too long, for it was responded sooner than I had expected, for My father left me a memorandum upon his demise. That memorandum is still with me until this moment. It never left my pocket.'

My companion paused for a couple of seconds to take out this note he talked about and asked, 'Would you like to hear it?' It was an oratorical query for, he had started reading out the note, indifferent for my response. The words of the father that left his son unaccompanied in this grotesque world contained deep affection for his son that even I, who didn't know this man, felt through his words as my companion recited them.

"My cherished son,"

"I know you have a lot of queries that ought to be answered. Do not worry, they will be upon reading this note. I do not want you to feel any sort of sorrow. You are my son, and I do not want you to ever believe that I did this horrible act for I am feeble. Your old man had to do this for your own good. Let me elucidate what

I mean in these last words of mine that I hope would make any vagueness illuminate".'

'"Just before I met your mother, I was living in England. You did not know this fact for I never wanted you to know. In England, I was making my living as a burglar. A professional burglar. My burgling dexterities were not as remarkable as the one who planned them. My son, I would like to introduce you to the man who is the dearest to your father after yourself, Professor James Moriarty. He helped your father pass his demanding times, and he is the centre of the spider web, the leader of the organisation I worked in. Without his aid, I was never going to be the man I am today. If you are asking yourself, "how did he help you when we were living in poverty in Australia?" then I must tell you this, my son. If it was not for him, your father would have been dead a long time ago".'

'"As I was saying, just before I met your mother, I was a burglar in London. In fact, the most famous burglar at that time. In one semi-successful burglary, I left a clue that would have led the yard to my route. I, therefore, upon Professor Moiety's order, sailed to Australia upon the hope of getting away. I had to live in poverty to remain low for some years until the tension dropped. I had waited for a letter from the organisation for years, until it finally arrived and the tension for my hunt had dropped. I took you with me back to London, and we lived a peaceful life until a man with the Professor's same level of intellect stood in front of him. This man's name is Sherlock Holmes, and he is the reason for making us drop a dozen attempted burglaries for he would have been easily able to track us. He stood side to side with Moriarty. I frequently heard rumours in the organisation, saying that Sherlock Holmes is his arch-nemesis. It was either be the hunter or the prey. If the organisation did not attempt to move him out of our road, he would've connected every murder, theft, and forgery case to our organization. And so, the professor stated that he is the only man eligible to stand in front of him. Last week, on the 5th of May was the day that Professor Moriarty was going to end Sherlock Holmes by pushing him off Reichenbach Falls in Switzerland. He *anticipated Sherlock Holmes coming to Switzerland to cross his plans once more. I would have never imagined the incident of that day. I did not doubt our leader's plans for a second. The amount of desolation my conscious received was a severe one. Professor James Moriarty, our solid brick, fell off the Reichenbach Falls alongside his arch-nemesis Sherlock Holmes. Upon my saviour's death, the organisation collapsed, and other organisations that were hunting my name some years ago were after me again. They had made a murder attempt upon me already. I knew that if they figured out that I had a son, they would have done what I do not want to envision. So, I had to take matters into my own hands. Do not shed a tear son, your old man does not have any regrets. Live your life to the fullest and follow my leader's, Professor James Moriarty, footsteps and take vengeance upon Sherlock Holmes. Avenge your father and the organisation. I hope you understand the situation I was confronted in, my son".'*

-With deep affection, your father, Vandican"'

Upon narration of the note, he folded it back, putting it back into his pocket while saying 'The motive you ask yourself? A mere vengeance, that is my motive. Still in the gloom? Let me elucidate. I am Mr Moriarty's pupil. My sole goal is to avenge him. I have been searching for Sherlock Holmes's successor for as long as I can remember. The idea of buying the most iconic place in Baker Street and waiting for my prey to come to me instead of me to it came to mind. I was in cold storage waiting for someone with the cerebral mind of the great Sherlock Holmes so that I could avenge Mr Moriarty, England's most iconic criminal mastermind. The Napoleon of crime.'

'Upon my father's request, I took Mr Moriarty's footsteps and started learning increasingly about his methodology and intellect. He has been my professor that my thoughts work upon even though I have not met him.

My great abhorrence towards Sherlock Holmes was incomparable. You don't realize the felicity I was in when you arrived at Baker Street.'

'I worked out this plan from the first day you had arrived. I wanted to see just how much of Sherlock Holmes cells you have gotten into you, and if you get to solve the mystery, then you're indeed his successor, and I would take vengeance upon you afterwards. I knew that that incompetent Robert would fail to act upon his part. You were correct, he was going to betray me just as a lion betrays his master. He wanted me to help him get reprisal. Paradoxically that he had to die down his own road.'

'I must admit, I am indeed impressed, and you are indeed a pupil of his just as I am of the Professor, but to your lack of providence, no one will approve the words of only a person accusing another of murder. No one heard our conversation, and after we finish discussing this business, I will make sure to take diligent care of my boot. I must thank you for this clue you have given to me.'

'You are quite confident. Aren't you?'

'Why shouldn't I be?'

'It's a shame… Alas, you had to murder four innocent individuals with no motive at all. A mere vengeance, you say? A person only lives once. How can you use human lives as a mere game?'

'You will come to realise my perspective when your life's objective is on the line.'

'I thought that we would make a good company. Alas, you had to be apprehended this soon.'

'What are you talking about? Did you comprehend what I was saying? You have no ev—'

'Inspector, pray, come out of the closet.'

EPISODE XVIII:
THE FINAL
PROBLEM

'**I**nspector, pray, come out of the closet.' Upon cry-
ing these words, my companion's face altered from
a self-assured one to the most cynical one that admitted
defeat.

'Richard Vandican, you are arrested for being the mastermind behind the murder of Charles S- and Robert
Anderson and for the murder of Terry H- and Cecil II.'
Cried the inspector simultaneously after coming out of
the closet.

'It looks like the adventure I have chosen has taken
part in my downfall' declared my companion showing
his disappointment.

'What story?' I asked.

'The Dying Detective', replied my companion.

'Oh, that's atypical.'

'If I remember correctly, you did not yet tell me yet what was wrong with my part of the story. Care to enlighten me if you still remember?' Asked my companion while the inspector was putting the cuffs on his hands.

'Well if I remember correctly, the first mistake was that it wasn't in October but November. The second was that the planter visited London from Sumatra. I do not quite remember what you said, but I am sure it was something else. The third one I, unfortunately, don't recall.'

'Your help is much appreciated, Mr Joy. I am sure we will consult you if any difficulties befall us, but you! You Vandican! How can you do such a thing!' cried the inspector as he grasped my companion by his elbow and walked towards the door.

'It's a pity, Mr Joy' declared my companion while pausing in his tracks and rotating so that he is now facing me. With a look on my friend's face that I did not quite recognise he cried, 'You have brought destruction upon me…I shall do as much to you.'

There was a moment of silence. I turned my face towards the window, grinned to myself, and replied, 'I will cheerfully accept the latter.'

…END…

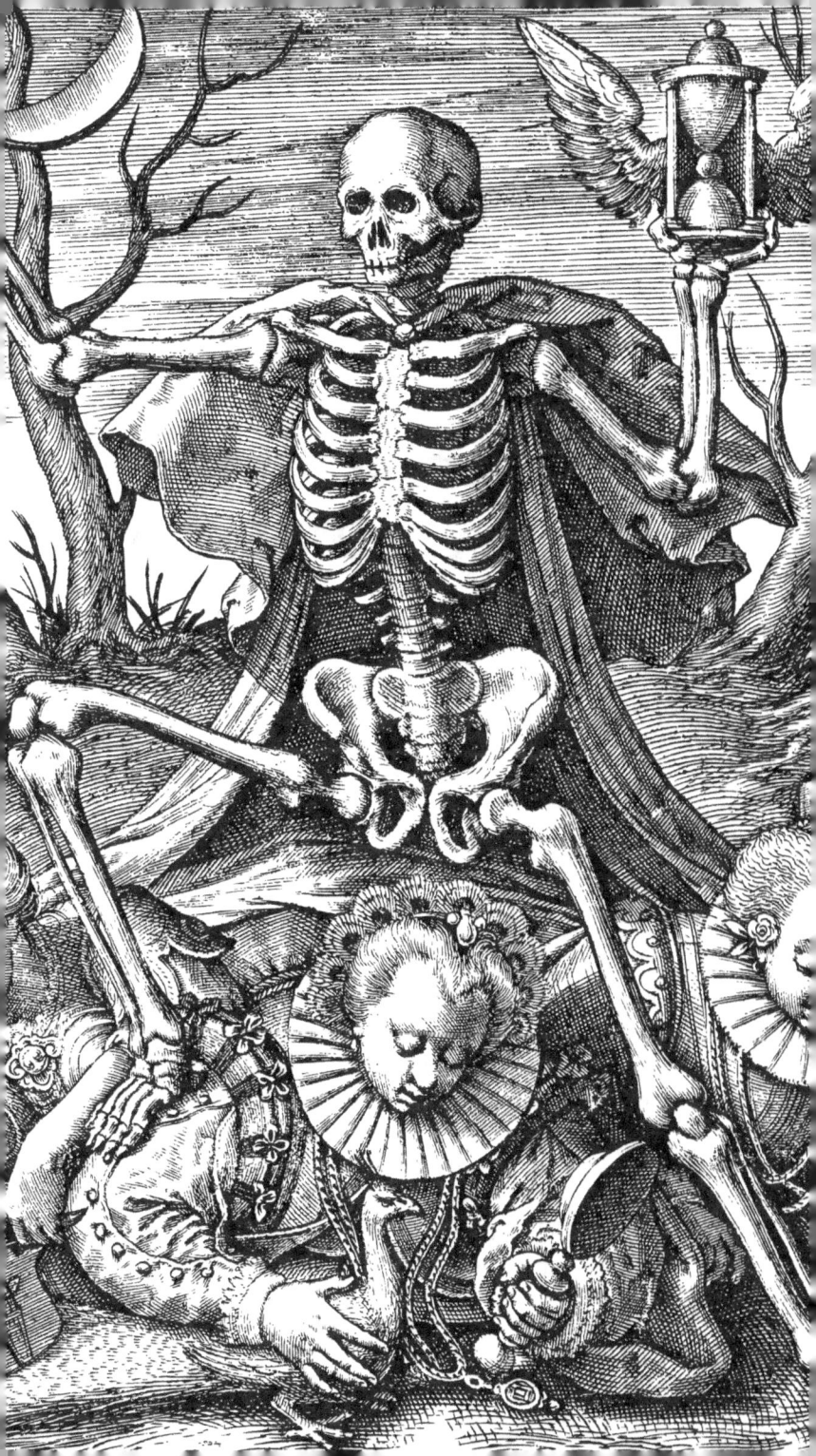

THE ADVENTURE OF THE VENGEFUL ONE

SPRING I

"Ahhh", sighed Williams as he straightened his back and stretched his arms while sitting on his desk in 221b Baker Street. It was half-past ten, yet he sighed and felt sleepy. Williams had been working on his Sherlock Holmes monograph, regarding the art of disguise, all night. In briefness, the monograph examined how any disguise is not whole with garments merely. One must use the speaking skills, the muscle memory skills, and most importantly, the acting skills of his subject of disguise in order to fully master the art of disguise. While writing his monograph, Williams had not noticed the passing of the night. 'That's enough for today. May as well carry on with it once I wake up', thought Williams while trying to figure out how to arrange the dispersed papers on his desk filled with ideas included in the monograph. 'Perhaps I ought to just toss away the ones I included and retain the others.'

It took Williams about two-quarters of an hour to categorise his papers. After regretting the initiation of this action, he started moving towards the settee to satisfy his eyes with a slight dose of sleep, otherwise he won't be able to work. 'Did I just hear a knock on the door or was it my weary mind playing games on me?' thought Williams and wished for the latter. 'Mr Joy, are you there?' Williams sighed after realising it was the Landlord bringing yet another client. 'I'm there indeed. If there is a client who wants to meet me, tell him that I already have a client.'

'He states that he's an acquaintance of yours, Mr Joy, and that it is an utmost urgency to meet you', replied the landlord before Williams could even take another step towards the settee. Williams changed his gaze from the settee towards the door, assuming it was merely another one of his clients using needless words. 'Right, what's his name?' asked Williams with a drained look on his face.

'He says his name is Jack. Mr Jack Barnes. Apparently, he's a sailor who worked with you on a cargo ship last autumn', replied the Landlord. Williams closed his eyes and searched through his memories for a man named Jack Barnes. Not even a second of thought had passed, when Williams opened his eyes as if a dose of energy flew inside his body. 'Pray, bring him in. You should have stated his name from the commencement', demanded Williams as he went around the room, tidying it for his guest. Finally, after managing to make the room appear somewhat adequate, he seated himself on his armchair and waited patiently for his friend. After a couple of seconds, the Landlord opened the door for Williams' guest to step inside. 'Williams! My dear old mate. How have ya been this past year?' cried the guest, or perhaps Mr Jack, as he walked towards Williams while stretching his arms to give him a manly embrace.

'Barnes! Dear old fella. I have been brimming with exhilaration. Tell me about yours!' replied Williams with eagerness as he embraced Mr Barnes. 'Pray, take a seat and tell me about your life in this past year', asked Williams while having his hand upstretched towards the seat in front of his desk.

'Thus far it has been great! Acquired myself a nice household with a complimentary garden in the countryside for retirement', answered Mr Barnes as he took a seat and glanced towards Williams.

'Not surprised! You always gabbed about gardens. Good God! You even took care of different kinds of plants back in our cabin!'

'Indeed, indee-...' replied Mr Barnes, but before he could continue, Williams interrupted him.

'Mr Henderson, pray bring a drink for my dear friend if you may' asked Williams of the landlord while gesturing with his hands.

'No, no. Don't mind me. I just came to discuss an urgent matter with you, Williams. Nothing more. In fact, I came to discuss the incident that occurred last fall...', stated Mr Barnes halting the Landlord from his tracks.

'I perceive, if my train of thought is right, that you suspect a behind the scenes crime syndicate behind the vanishing of the ship's business.' ...

There was a moment of silence in the room. From the look of Mr Barnes' expression, he was in utter perplexity as to how Williams deduced the exact idea, he came to see him for. 'Good heavens, Williams! How did you come to this conclusion?' asked Mr Barnes placing both his palms on the armchair to show his eagerness to know the answer.

'Compose yourself, my dear friend. It was a simple train of thought, nothing more. From the moment I heard your name and utter urgency, my memory took me to last fall's incident impulsively. As you entered my flat, I immediately noticed your bad tendency of unfastening your last two chemise buttons when you are in a state of deep thinking or concern. How I came to the conclusion that you deduced a behind the scenes crime syndicate was quite simple. In fact, I myself did an investigation regarding the incident and came to quite a similar conclusion. Once you mentioned that you came to discuss last fall's incident, everything simply fell into place', answered Williams.

'Urrmm… Mr Williams, Mr Barnes… I apologise for the interruption of your discussion, but I was exceedingly curious to hold myself back. Just what occurred last autumn?' asked the Landlord while stepping inside the flat as he saw Williams gesturing and giving him the permission to do so.

'Do not bother to apologise mate. It's an incident worth hearing and storytelling. Ain't that right Williams?' asked Mr Barnes Williams rhetorically, 'take a seat, we have plenty of time. I will tell-tale ya the incident that occurred last fall', declared Mr Barnes, but before he could launch into his narration of the incident, Williams restrained him, 'Hold on my dear friend. I have written the incident in detail as a chronicle. It should be around here somewhere', said Williams, as he was looking through the pile of stories and manuscripts placed near the window. 'Here it is!' exclaimed Williams in relief and satisfaction, 'Mr Henderson, pray, why don't you narrate this manuscript out loud so that Mr Barnes here can correspondingly hear it too', asked Williams to the Landlord as he walked towards him to hand the manuscript.

'With pleasure, sir. It has been a tradition to read your manuscripts now. Is it satisfactory for you, sir, Mr Barnes, if we advance with this method?' asked the landlord while looking amid the manuscript and Mr Barnes.

'No hitch at all mate. I'm a fan of Williams' stories and monographs in truth. Used to read his works back in our cabin', replied Mr Barnes as he adjusted his seat in a more comfortable position.

'Right then. Pray Mr Henderson, proceed with the chronicle,' asked Williams while comforting and shutting his eyes in concentration.

...

THE INCIDENT THAT OCCURRED LAST AUTUMN!

FALL

The chronicle you are about to examine goes back to an autumn season when I was 18 years of age. Sorry to say, I did not take up university for I was not eager enough to devote myself to a systematic establishment. Thence, I ended up working alongside my father on cargo ships as a sailor and a cook, later to the degree of a third mate. It has now been six months since I started working alongside my father, who has the rank of a chief officer, in order save enough money to achieve my goal which is to dedicate my life to the art of deduction. The name of the ship we were working under at the time was Motor Vessel "Lion". And indeed, it was an accurate name for such a ship with an age below ten years and a cargo holding capacity of ten thousand tons.

Returning to our matter, the main state of affairs we were under was that we just finished the "loading of cargo operation" from the Port of Runavik, Norway and were on our way to the Port of Southampton, United Kingdom in instruction to discharge the cargo. To be more precise, the cargo we were loading was steel billets. At this point in time, we just sailed out of Norway and were on our way to the United Kingdom…

'All right boys. It appears that the meteorological conditions will get nasty this evening. Let us haste inside and have our supper', ordered the cadet captain watching us from the bridge.

'Let's get back inside', Jack Barnes, my Irish cabin mate told me, 'A storm is approaching, I reckon.'

'I do hope your sixth sense is wrong this time', I replied, as I followed him inside to the kitchen table where supper was prepared. 'Williams, everything's in order? The holds are secured?' asked my father while handing me a plate.

'sealed and secured! No concerns.' As we were beginning to eat our supper, Ben and James, our third and second officers, entered the kitchen. 'I'm telling ya mate, Hudson is the upcoming heavyweight champ. Ain't that right Williams?' asked Ben as he held a plate in his hand and approached the table.

'My dear friend. Even if I'm a middleweight, I can outbox any heavyweight boxer out there!' I replied light-heartedly while looking at my three crew-mates entering the kitchen. More precisely, our third second, and chief engineers.

'Aye, Williams! Let us have a sparring after supper!' exclaimed James with food in his mouth.

'I am prepared at any-...', I replied but couldn't conclude my reply for the captain's words overwhelmed mine, 'Alright boys, weather's not looking good. Ben, go check the ropes' security as usual after supper.'

'Aye, Aye, captain!'

'I will go along with him to hasten the checking for it seems it started pouring outside.' ...

...

Following supper, mostly all of the crew-members stayed behind in the kitchen to have some leisure time with the anomaly of Ben and James for evident reasons, the captain who went back up to the bridge, and the engineers who went back down to the engine room. 'Say Williams, let's play a game mate. One has to describe a Sherlock Holmes story using three words while the other has to deduce the title of that story', Implied Jack eagerly. We used to play this game quite ordinarily in our cabin if we had any leisure time on our hands. I enjoyed beating him at his own game, therefore, I answered while turning my gaze towards him, 'Well, my friend, the game is afoot!' A couple of moments passed in silence for my friend was attempting to deduce the title of the story with the phrase I just uttered. Once my friend's expression straightened with self-assurance, he turned his gaze towards me, 'You know I don't require any warmups, Williams! Who do you think you are talking to mate? I have read the stories over a dozen times now. The answer is, "The Adventure of the Abbey Grange" of course', replied my friend with a grin which expressed his feeling of overwhelmingness.

'Just testing your memory as I initially do. Now do proceed, you have indeed got it correct', I replied and waited for him to come up with his three words.

'All right mate, as you say. Let me contemplate', replied Jack as he proceeded to untie his chemise's two upper buttons. 'Howl, silence, and bewildering', answered my friend with a grin, same as the previous one, filled with every ounce of self-assurance, 'Try to deduce that!'

'Shadowing your train of thought, an answer to my deduction is the famous maxim "don't judge a book by its cover"-…'

'Just state your answer, Williams!' interrupted Jack impatiently.

'The Adventure of Silver Blaze', I answered while making eye contact with my friend. Looking puzzled, he replied, 'Dhy did y-…'

'As I said', I interrupted him, 'If you would have let me carry on with my elucidation, you would have known. In briefness, I have put myself in your train of thoughts and went by your logic on how you would try to mislead me', I finally answered his bewilderment.

'All right mate, all right. Quit your grinning. Mr Joy, I see you're having a laugh, wanna join us?' asked Jack to my father as he saw him having a giggle watching us.

'I will go and have a check on the boys. They seem to have taken quite a while, and it's raining and growing dark outside', replied my father as he walked out of the kitchen. As my friend distinguished, there was no point in replying back to my father as he returned his gaze towards me. 'Go on, mate. Come up with something', I turned my gaze towards the window to run over my memory files involving Mr Holmes' stories. 'I think this one will do', I thought to myself and turned my gaze back towards my friend, 'Anticipation, patience, and insignificance', I asked Jack and instantly, a face of bewilderment aroused on his face after hearing my words.

'Are you solemn?' He asked.

'Absolutely!'

He took his time to reply. He Gazed towards the sealing to come up with ideas but alas, from the look he had on his face, his train of thought wasn't in accordance with mine. Finally, he said, 'I give up. I can't think of anything… What is the answer?'

'Well, my friend, if y-…' Before I could provide him with the answer, both of us were held captivated by the echo of my father's shouting of my name. My heart sank inside my chest. I thought something mischievous occurred to him, and it seems that Jack thought the same for we both got up at the same moment to go outside. Before we took a step, my father was already in the kitchen. It seemed that the shouting echoed through the room, which made it seem like he was far away. 'What's wrong? What occurred?' I asked impatiently while looking concerned.

'James… Oh good gracious…' My father replied. By the expression on his face, something grotesque must have had occurred. When I observe my surroundings, I realised that something was off, 'Where is James? What had occurred to him?' I asked both Ben and my father. Both of them looked at each other in speechlessness, and then my father replied, 'James died. He slipped and fell into the ocean. We were hopeless with this rain and darkness outside. Oh, God!' answered my father while expressing distress.

'Father come take a seat. It's okay. Do not stress yourselves. We will go bring the others, and then you can recall what had occurred in detail.' His answer came as a thunderbolt for me, at least. Such a grotesque incident to take place was quite distressing. After I seized a seat for my father to sit on, Jack and I went to gather the rest of the crew-members.

…

'All right, Mr Joy, please proceed and tell us what has occurred without upsetting yourself', assured the captain my father, who was drinking sips from the liquor bottle. Although liquor is prohibited on ships, some exceptions are made.

'I was in the kitchen when I realised that the boys, Ben and James, seemed to take a while to check the ropes' security, so I went to have a look outside. When I stepped outside, I heard a slight voice of someone shouting. Going 'round the corner, I saw Ben's back as he was leaning and holding James' hand screaming 'Don't let go!' When I reached them, it was regrettably too late… James had vanished… If… If only I got there earlier to help Ben hold onto James…'

'Now, it ain't your fault, Mr Joy. Don't stress yourself over the matter. You need to compose yourself as much as you can at such times', replied the captain in an attempt to support him. He turned his gaze towards Ben, who gave the impression of being just as distressed as my father, 'Big boy, what has occurred?' asked the captain. Ben, still gazing onto the ground replied, 'We were checking the ropes, and the rain started getting heavier. Therefore, I naturally turned towards James to instruct him to work with cautiousness. Then, that was when I saw him slipping on one of the ropes on the ground and going over the steel barrier. I swear I moved as fast as I could to hold on to him but… but…' Ben couldn't endure the burden of continuing his sentence and fell into his own stream of tears.

'You're a big fella. Don't distress yourself. It ain't your fault', continued the captain in an attempt to the crew-mates' morale, 'All of us, let us hold a moment of silence for James. We need to stay strong together.' It was quite distressing even though I wasn't acquainted with James that well; I still considered him a friend, nevertheless. The rest of the night went on without much tête-à-tête between us—just silence. Nobody understood or perhaps grasped the incident that had befallen us…

…

I typically am one of the early risers. That is, of course, regarding normal shifts for there are crew-members who have night shifts and sleep during the day. Only during supper and breakfast do all the crew-members get together. I, as usual, woke up at sunrise to prepare breakfast, which takes me about three-quarters of an hour. 'Mornin' Mate', exclaimed Jack as he entered the cabin for he had just finished his shift. He ordinarily comes with me in the kitchen to prepare breakfast and sleeps afterwards. 'Morning, Jack. I am set. Let's head to the kitchen.'

'The whole matter feels more of a daydream. Did James really die…' thought Jack and sounded like he directed his words towards the empty space instead of me. I kept silent for I had no words of reply for such an unfathomable query. 'Williams, do you think he went to heaven?' asked Jack in the hope of a positive answer in order to satisfy his inner conflict.

'God made him blunder in the first place. In a way he, she, or whatever God has technically murdered him. Objectively, God should grant James heaven by his teachings. Subjectively, God works in mysterious way. That's, of course, if a God is up there or down there in the first place', I replied to Jack's question. I was talking more to myself than answering the question. I noticed Jack's expression of bewilderment but pretended overlook it.

'What in the name of heavens are you on about?' asked Jack in bewilderment.

'Nothing nothing. Just dazing off.'

'Let's just start preparing breakfast', replied my friend. And, therefore, off we started preparing the breakfast. Halfway through preparing the breakfast, the second engineer dashed in the kitchen and out of breath, 'It's Warel, the third engineer, we cannot find him anywhere. He simply disappeared!' cried the third engineer, 'I gave the notice about his disappearance to the captain and all the other crew-members. I don't understand what is occurring! Yesterday James, now Warel!'

'Take a seat and compose yourself. Are the crew-members coming to the kitchen?' I advised and asked the second engineer, who looked completely distressed.

'Yes. They should come down anytime soon', answered the second engineer while taking a tissue and wiping off the sweat on his forehead.

'Right, I will go and check Warel's cabin in the meantime. Wait for the others here, you two.' I shouted as I hurried up the stairs in the direction of Warel's cabin. I opened the door, and surprisingly, it was open. I stepped inside, hoping I might find a clue which might help clarify his sudden disappearance. I looked through his room from his closet to his bed-sheets, but nothing! The cabin was absolutely ordinary. I was merely looking for a small detail which might optimistically lead me to a clarification for Warel's sudden disappearance.

'I moved towards his desk to take a look around. Papers relating to the ship's engine room were spread all over his desk. Observing closely, a thunderbolt of insight pierced right through my body which gave me a hint regarding Warel's sudden disappearance. On Warel's desk was an important clue regarding his disappearance-… 'Williams, everyone's in the kitchen waiting for you mate. Let's go!' I heard Jack's voice behind my back which brought an end to my flow of thoughts and concentration.

'Right. Let's hurry to the kitchen then…' I replied as I turned my back and walked towards him.

'Did you find anything that might help us?' asked Jack as we were going down the stairs.

'Perhaps. But now's not the time to be discussing such matters', I answered as we entered the kitchen to find all the crew-members grouped, just as yesterday.

'All right boys. Now, I don't quite understand the second engineer. What do you mean Warel disappeared?' asked the captain while taking control of the situation for most of the crew-members were chattering with each other in distress.

'He simply vanished into thin air. The last time I saw him was yesterday in the engine room when he notified me that he would take a nap. Since then, there was no sign of him. I went to his room this morning for my shift was over, but he was nowhere to be seen. I looked throughout the ship, and I still couldn't get a hold of him', replied the second engineer in distress and agitation.

'Compose yourself big man. Maybe you do not recall that he had left you a notice about his current whereabouts. In addition to yesterday's incident, I wouldn't be surprised if you wouldn't recall', suggested the captain to the second engineer although the second engineer still insisted on Warel's disappearance as being disturbing.

'I'm telling ya. Something is going on. Some incidents are occur-…'

'I… I've read about this in the papers a couple of days back! It stated h… how cargo ships are vanishing one after the other, along with their crew-members! It must be the curse of the ocean! It will swallow us all!' cried Ben in distress and out of control.

'Ben, big boy! Compose yourself mate', the captain ordered Ben as he walked towards him in order to help compose him.

'I can't! We will all vanish!' Ben kept shouting while taking a seat back on the table. Every other crew-member was speechless. Distress was visible on every crew-member's face. Observing the crew-members' expressions, I decided that an intervention was required in order to help raise their morale, 'There are a couple of accounts we can come up with, at the present time, regarding Warel's disappearance:

'**[1]** The first theory that clarifies Warel's disappearance is that, for whatever reason, he decided to step outside in the rain and wind where evidently, he might have had the same fate as James. He may even have had some liquor for everyone seemed distressed yesterday and most noticeably him. Obviously, alcohol with rain don't go together. I'm distressed as much as you are currently, but Warel might be beyond our help if indeed this theory is correct…'

'Williams! What are you muttering about!? That's imp-…'

'Let him finish what he has started', interrupted the captain to the second engineer's revolt and gestured to me to recommence, **[2]** As for the second elucidation or theory, Warel may perhaps be currently located aboard with us in a space we have yet looked for.

'**[3]** The third theory is the mere fact that we don't know. In which case, for all three theories or elucidations, the course of action that is necessary for us to undertake is to compose, maintain, and continue our work as customarily for there is no other rational action we can take at the moment. And therefore gentlemen, in order to regain our composure, I suggest having breakfast...' I finally suggested to the crew-members.

Silence fell upon the room for it was an experience neither one of us had undergone before. My father, as luck would have it, finally replied, 'I think it is a pleasant suggestion. We need to alleviate our minds from the past incidents until we arrive in the United Kingdom.'

'How can we just forget about Wa-...' cried the second engineer in protest but the captain placed his palm on his shoulder in order to compose him and suggest having some breakfast.

...

And thus, we had breakfast, and everyone went along to pick up again his ordinary labour. Glaring through the window at the rain, wind, and weather, I thought to myself, 'We have to merely overlook the fact that two of our crew-members died and went missing in the course of ten hours. I don't believe in superstitions but from the expression upon the faces of my crew-members, especially Ben, implied that they considered some sort of curse had been cast upon the ship at the moment. Although I have an initial hint concerning what is occurring, I am not quite certain yet...'

I felt, at that point in time, as if I'm at the gist of the cosmos. I felt trivial yet perceived Vastness. I imagined myself in another part of the world without a care in the world. Experiencing another life within a sunny world... Actuality, for a trice, felt comical and peculiar...

...

It was half past five, and I was in the kitchen preparing supper, 'Say Williams, what is the answer for yesterday's game?' asked Jack as he entered the kitchen, 'I have been thinking for an answer all day long, but I constantly fail to come up with one.'

'Don't inform me you hadn't had any sleep just for the sake of coming up with an answer', I exclaimed and turned my gaze towards him.

'Just answer the question before anything else barges in and interrupts us.'

'Right. "The Adventure of the Red-Headed League". Satisfied?' I asked with a grin while placing the plates on the table.

'Wh... Oh, of course... I feel rather half-witted now. It was relatively palpable', replied Jack with a satisfied and relieved expression... As the both of us were placing supper on the plates, the echoes of footsteps emerged from the hallway. 'We will also need to work on the piston as mentioned before...' emerged the voice's holder into the kitchen, disclosing his identity as the chief engineer discussing some matter with the captain and my father, 'Let's leave all the modification until our arrival to the United Kingdom', replied the captain as he took a seat on the table, 'All right, who are we still waiting for to start supper? Where are Ben and the second engineer?'

'Aye, Aye, Captain', came the immediate reply from the second engineer as if he was waiting for the captain to call upon him.

'Good, take your seat. Where is Ben?' asked the captain while looking at us.

'May possibly be in his cabin. Will go and have a look', replied Jack and he instantaneously got up from his seat and proceeded to his proposed task.

'Williams, I will require you to check the ropes' security from now on for the obvious motives. Are you up for it?' asked, or more so ordered, the captain of me. I couldn't refuse even if it was a selection of my choice. We were short of essentially needed crew-members by two, the crew-member's morale was in distress and agitation, and there was no other crew-member up for the job for each one had his work rate doubled after the incidents.

'Aye, Aye captain!' Came my immediate reply with enthusiasm as an effort to raise the morale amongst the crew-mates. At this point, everyone remained in uncommunicativeness. A couple of minutes passed since Jack went to look for Ben and yest there was no sign of him nor Ben. 'Williams, go check what the boys are doing and what's holding them back from coming', asked my father. 'Go on and do what your father asked Williams', came the approval of the captain for my father's order as I was walking towards to commence my provided task.

'Jack! Ben!' I raised my voice from down the stairs as I was calling their names. I went until the second floor where Ben's cabin was situated, 'Jack! BEN!'… Total silence. The shadows of uneasiness crept behind my mind. I couldn't understand why would this kind of feeling arise so abruptly. I was facing Ben's cabin door at this point. I started raising my arm to open the door. An action of five seconds felt like an eternity. I finally managed to place my palm on the doorknob. I opened the door while sweat was dripping from my chin… No one… There was no one in the room. 'Merely my imagination, huh?' I thought to myself. I raised both my arms to my mouth as to shout for Jack and Ben, yet again, in the hope of an answer from either one of them, JACK! B-...'

'Stop shouting mate! My earbuds are sensitive!' cried Jack from the bridge's room as he was coming down. A sense of relief rushed through me. I was happy that my superstitions were on the side of their definition, mere superstitions. 'Good Apollo Jack! Where have you been? I've been looking for you fellows!' I replied with a satisfied voice, but after seeing the weary expression upon Jack's face, the uneasy feeling grasped my body in its palms of shadow once again. 'Wha... What the matter, Jack?' I asked in disorientation.

'It's bloody Ben Williams! I can't find him anywhere!' cried Jack with desperation, 'I looked everywhere. Thought he might still be upstairs on the bridge but there ain't any sign of him!'

'Boys... What is going on upstairs? Come to the kitchen', cried my father from downstairs. Both of us glanced at one another. Both speechless and leadless concerning the course of action we should approach this situation with.

'Let's clarify the situation in the kitchen to the captain and crew-mates', suggested Jack while looking down the stairs. Agreeing to his suggestion, I proceeded to go down the stairs.

...

'Are you really suggesting that Ben disappeared? Is that what you're suggesting?' asked the captain in a state of disbelief, as if trying to convince himself that what is occurring is just in his imagination.

'Aye, captain! Searched everywhere but he was nowhere to be found!' answered Jack with irritation for he answered this question a dozen times in the space of twenty-four hours.

'IT'S THE CURSE! This is the ocean's curse! We will all vanish into the ocean!' cried the second engineer with desperation while placing his palms on his temples.

'I agree with him! I've read through the newspaper that discussed the topic of the curse. IT'S REAL. Ships have disappeared. What if we are one of these ships!' the chief engineer stated, backing the words of the second engineer. The situation started to grow out of hand. The expression on each crew-mate showcased one topic which was the desperation for survival.

Thankfully, our appointed captain was one with the skill of taking control of situations, 'Everyone, Stop with the nonsense! Now let's return the plates and start to search for Ben. All the crew-members will search inside the ship for Ben and Warel! Didn't you hear me, boys!? ON YOUR FEET AND START THE SEARCH!' cried the captain, ordering everyone. His voice gave a chill throughout our bodies for everyone was on his feet as soon as the captain started to raise his voice. Every crew-member placed his plate in the refrigerator and went on to commence the search. Before Jack and I were able to commence the search, the captain gestured for us to stop in our tracks, 'Boys. I want you to look for them outside. There ain't no other person I can entrust this task with but you. Take care, and if you take more than a quarter of an hour, I'm coming for you!'

'Aye, Aye Captain!' came our reply immediately as we changed our tracks from inside to the outside of the ship. The atmosphere surrounding the ship resembled the extraction of light while the insertion of a shadow of darkness and bloodlust grasped the ship. 'Will we be able to survive? Do curses truly exist?' I kept thinking to myself at the time. The rain detained our sights to their minimal potential. We searched amid the hold's hatches but, predictably, no leads were found. I observed around at my surroundings for any place where leads might be found, and to my relief, there was. I hiked with caution towards the crane which was positioned at the right half of the ship. Thence, I had to go all around the ship to reach the crane.

Once I reached my destination, I started climbing the crane's steps when I realised that the crane's door was actually closed. Consequently, I naturally wouldn't be able to get inside, so there was no point in climbing in the first place. When I placed my foot back on the ground, everything from James' incident to the disappearances was revealed in a thunderbolt of realisation. Revealed in a way as if I'm behind the magician on a stage, watching the trick taking place knowing full well the magician's trick. The only thing holding me back was the percentage, even if minimal, of being mistaken. I had to come up with a plan in order to bring an end to this curse…

'Williams! LET'S GET BACK INSIDE!' cried Jack from the other side while waiting for my approval. I gestured with my hands the approval, and in the next instance, we rushed back inside. Once we stepped inside, we realised how much the temperature inside differs from the one outside. Water spread from our garments and bodies on the ground as if a wave of water once the door opened. Instead of searching for Ben and Walter, we felt that we went for a swim in the ocean and came back inside. 'All right boys. By the appearance on ya faces, I would say nothing was found. In any case, it was an expected result. Rush! Change your garments and get back to the kitchen.' The captain's order echoed through the stairs as we rushed to get changed upon his orders.

...

'It seems like there is something occurring in the ship and I finally decided to address it directly', continued the captain, 'First of all, there ain't any curse on the ship. There must be some logical explanation for these incidents. Thus, make sure you lock your cabin's doors just in case. Going outside the ship is prohibited until either the weather gets better or we arrive at the port of discharge. The second engineer will have to continue filling Warel's engine report, Williams will check the ropes' security from now on, and finally, Mr Joy, you would need to triple your work effort so that it will fill Ben's and James' work. Of course, if you need any help from Jack or Williams, make sure to ask them. If all is understood, let us proceed to resume our supper and return to our labour', concluded the captain, and as per orders, we proceeded to place the plates on the table. 'I will eat my supper. You won't have to wash my plate afterwards, Williams!' stated Jack as we were placing the plates on the table.

'Why?' I asked jokingly while taking a seat on the table.

'You ask why? We haven't eaten even breakfast mate! I'm famished-…' Thanks to Jack's phrase, I realised at that exact moment the plan I was looking for to end this curse occurring on the ship.

'Williams? What's amiss mate? Go on, eat your portion of food aren't you famished?' asked Jack, seeing me dazing off in my train of thoughts

'Wha… What did you just say!?' I asked again with the flames of determination in my eyes.

'I… Beg your pardon? I'm hungry mate! Go on and eat your meal for God's sake.' answered Jack while stuffing his mouth with yet another spoon of food before he even gulped what was in his mouth.

'That's it! That's it!' I kept repeating to myself, 'This plan should work!'

...

After we ate supper, each crew-member went along to resume his labour while I stayed in the kitchen to wash the plates. My mind was occupied with coming up with a plan regarding the current situation. When holding the final plate I had to wash, the plan was finalised! 'Aye, mate. Please warm up the water for tea' asked Jack entering the kitchen with his mug in hand. Jack despised drinking from the same mug or cup like the others. I don't judge this tendency of his for I have the same distaste. 'Jack! On time! Enter and close the door behind, will you?' I asked Jack, 'Look here... We may face an adventure this night. Are you up for one?' I asked Jack while making eye contact.

'I don't understand what kind of adventure you're referring to but include me in, mate', Jack replied without a second of thought or a notion of what awaited him.

'Brilliant!' I exclaimed, 'The adventure is the following-...'

...

The time was around midnight. Every crew-mate was either in his cabin, in the bridge room, or in the engine room. In these places were the crew-member situated at the moment, which was quite well-known amongst us. I, who was supposed to be in my cabin, was waiting in the kitchen, more precisely, inside the storage room. Besides me was Jack who asked the captain for a change in the shifts for he was quite distressed and required relaxation. Of course, that was an excuse he used in order to join me. We were hiding in the storage room. Ordinarily, it would've been too cold to stand inside the storage room, but we took our coats with us. 'We have been waiting for two-quarters of an hour now, Williams! Just wh-…'

'Hushhh! Keep it down.' I whispered, 'I told you that you would have to trust me on this one. They will surely sho-…' Before I could resume my sentence, the sounds of footsteps echoed from the hallway to our ears. The footsteps kept getting closer. The footsteps entered the kitchen now. From the intensity of the moment, sweat started to form on our foreheads. I turned my gaze towards Jack, who gestured with his fingers a number sequence. I understood his intention. On the count of three, we would surprise our visitors.

1…

2…

3!

'Hold it right there!' I cried. However, observing closing, I realised the grave mistake which I committed when we opened the storage's door and laid our eyes on our visitor.

'Williams? What are you lads doing in the storage room?' asked the second engineer as he was holding a plate in his hands.

'Heaven's! Keep quiet! Leave the plate on the table and come inside right now!' I whispered. Without questioning my intentions, the second engineer followed my orders, and we were back inside the storage room.

'What is occurring Williams?! Jack!?' asked the second engineer in bewilderment while looking from one face to the other.

'Settle down. You will understand', answered Jack and gestured with his hands to hold still. Time passed yet nothing occurred. If my judgement was correct regarding my internal clock, I would say a quarter of an hour had passed since we re-entered the storage room. The second engineer's face grew grimmer in irritation. 'Lads! I'-...' As the second engineer started muttering his words, the sound of footsteps echoed, yet again, through the kitchen to enter our storage room.

Every ounce of muscle in our bodies remained motionless. These footsteps were obviously different from the one's Jack and I heard before. I turned my gaze towards Jack in order to see if he reached the same conclusion concerning the footsteps as myself. The second engineer's footsteps were quite carefree, which indicated him being indiscreet. But these footsteps were in a way sly. You could've imagined the person tiptoeing to the kitchen from the pattern of the echoes you heard. The footsteps reached the kitchen. Judging from our previous experience a couple of moments ago, I gazed back at Jack to start the number sequence.

1...

2...

... But before Jack managed to reach the count of 3, the second engineer rushed unexpectedly in front of us and opened the storage room's door. Before we even thought about his rashness, we were right behind the second engineer. 'Now. What is ha...' started the second engineer when he froze into place after observing the person standing in front of him. 'James!? Bu... But how!?' cried the second engineer while taking a few steps backwards in disbelief.

...

'Williams... Turns out like you were right. Yet again...' continued Jack, 'James, oh James. Now, where are Ben and Ware!?' ...

James stood in disbelief. He obviously had not fore-seen such an occurrence to take place. After realising the grave situation, he was in, digging his own grave, without a clue on how to explain himself, he collapsed on his knees in torment. 'Just tell me, how… how did you fig-ure out I'm alive? Ben advised me that the ploy worked on each one of you…' asked James in complete distress and disbelief.

'Williams! You knew, and you didn't mention anything to us!' cried the second engineer in irritation.

'Permit him to elucidate mate, and you will compre-hend' replied Jack while gesturing for me to start the elu-cidation as of how I came to the deduction that James was still alive.

'Right. Initially, I did not suspect anything for there would be no purpose to do so. I was as baffled, just as all the crew-members were, regarding your sudden death. No suspicions arose from me until you…' I explained while gesturing with my hand towards the second engi-neer, '…came into the kitchen and informed us about Warel's disappearance. Obviously, this is not something in the ordinary realm. I suspected some pulling of the strings behind the scenes.

'The idea of searching through Warel's cabin rushed through my mind, and so I hurried to his cabin to do so. At first, there was nothing in his cabin to disclose any-thing concerning his disappearance. But, after taking a closer look at his workspace, a piece of clue was available in front of my eyes which indicated that Warel was in the middle of an action, but something for some reason caused him to suddenly halt. That clue was his engine room report.'

'Of course! How could I have missed such a fact! Af-ter I took hold of the report, I realised it was half complete. But the notion that he stopped from completing the report for an alter reason hadn't crossed my mind.' cried the second engineer in hopelessness.

'The idea would have not come into your mind if you hadn't suspected anything in the first place, my dear. After realising that there was an external factor which halted Warel from resuming his work, a notion came to mind but I had not developed upon it then for I had to make sure Warel did in fact disappear. While we gathered with the crew-mates in the kitchen, I started to suspect Ben when he kept coming back to the 'curse of the ocean' tale. Something merely didn't feel right, but I couldn't describe what precisely.

'I forced myself to disregard my suspicions and regard Warel's disappearance as natural and unconnected to your death, James. But, as much as I tried suppressing my suspicions, my logical thoughts kept coming back. It was not until I met Jack in front of Ben's cabin and he informed me about the chances that Ben had joined Warel's disappearance that my suppression did break and I started thinking about an elucidation behind the incidents. As much as you looked at it, there was no denying that there was someone behind the curtains pulling the strings on the ship.

'At this point, only theories came to mind without concrete evidence. By then, Jack and I were outside the ship searching for Ben and Warel. Quite obviously, there was nothing to be found. But then, I started approaching the crane and attempted to climb it. Looking upwards I realised the crane's door was closed and that there was no way I could have entered inside. When I got back down, and the moment my foot touched the ground, everything fell into place. The crane's door is always kept open for the last person to leave the crane wouldn't be able to close it behind him. It is built in a way that it is only closed from the inside, which meant that someone must have been inside the crane at the time that I attempted to climb to take a look inside! Rationally, the only possible person or persons inside were Ben and or Warel, but I had four theories in mind:

'[1] The first notion in my mind was Ben being a serial murderer who had planned to murder all of us. [2] My second notion was that Ben and Warel were serial murderers and planned to murder all of us. Although this theory was somewhat doubtful for, why would Warel start writing his engine report if he planned to murder all of the crew-member in the first place? It would have been pointless.

'[3] I was not sure about this deduction for there was no evidence to support it, but, in any case, the theory was that the three of you, Ben, Warel, and yourself James, planned to murder all of us. Now, why would you murder all of us in the first place? The only logical reason to murder all the crew-members is that you either were vile homicidal criminal or you planned to steal the ship along with its cargo. But, from the mentioning of the ocean's curse nonsense and how ships vanish along with their crew-members by Ben, I thought the latter reason was the one to go with. You planned to frighten the crew-members with the ocean's curse and plant the fear inside their hearts to ease the murdering process.

'[4] My fourth and final notion was that you were just playing a joke on us. I hoped all my other notions were nonsense and that my 4th notion was the right theory, but I'm afraid, after seeing your reaction here and now, it appears that my third theory was the correct one.

'To return to your initial question of 'why was I in the storage room?', I simply thought of a plan as to how I can get a hold of you. When I was eating supper with Jack, he mentioned how much he was starving, and then, the obvious came to mind. If you were hiding inside the crane for so long, it was only rational that hunger would hit your stomachs eventually. My theory was that if all the crew-members knew where each and every one of the other crew-mates were situated at a given time along with their habits, it wouldn't be hard for you to sneak in the kitchen to get some food. Therefore, I, like yourselves, was familiar with the habit of the crew-members. And, around midnight, rarely did anyone approach the kitchen. Including the fact that I was sleeping, you had all the chances to sneak into the kitchen without being caught. And so, I asked Jack to hide with me in the storage room for I expected that one of you three would come to embezzle some food.' Finally concluding my analysis, a moment of silence in order for my words to sink in grasped the room.

Both, the second engineer and James, took quite a time to reflect the analysis. Jack already heard my analysis when I discussed with him the plan earlier during the day. The second engineer appeared to have returned to the present with us and asked, 'But, I still don't understand! How is James still alive?! Didn't your father witness him fall into the ocean?' Both Jack and James turned their gaze towards me.

It was a point I yet had to tackle, 'It was a visual deception. My father only mentioned seeing Ben's back leaning towards the steal barrier. He never mentioned actually seeing James falling into the ocean. James was already by that point, hiding inside the crane. James and Ben realised that if they took a long time to get inside, someone would eventually look for them. All Ben had to do was to wait for someone to show up outside and pretend that he is holding onto something from falling while shouting James' name. In addition to the fog and rain decreasing my father's visual potential, their plan to give the impression that James' had fallen into his death was bound to succeed.'

'But If what you're saying is that all they had to do is hide inside the crane, didn't the notion that someone might look inside the crane come to them?' asked the second engineer in disbelief.

'Besides myself, did any crew-mate decide to climb the crane during this storm? Brilliant, from your expression the answer is obviously no. They had planned to murder all of the crew-mates before anyone even thought about the crane' I answered while gazing from the second engineer to James. 'Now James, I deduce that Ben is inside the crane. Am I correct?'

'Heavens… Why did we decide to proceed with such an act? We have read in the papers an article that discussed how ships vanished into thin air. We thought it might be a good idea... We decided to hide inside the crane while murdering one crew-mate after another. The first was Warel. Ben knocked on his cabinet and asked him to step outside the ship to discuss something troubling him. Foolishly, Warel followed Ben outside. I knocked Warel on his head from behind, and we proceeded to throw Warel into the ocean afterwards. Our next plan was to plant the fear inside each crew-mate to ease the murdering process, but it seems that we have failed. It's just as you've analysed it. It's as if you were present with us at the moment we discussed our plan! We planned to sneak food while the crew-mates were doing their labour shift. I did n-…'

'James! Come on already! What is holding you so lo-…' suddenly, and out of nowhere, came the whispering of Ben, who by this point when he halted his whispering, was standing by the kitchen's door gazing at us, 'Oh, good heavens!' cried Ben and he proceeded to dash outside the ship. Jack instinctively proceeded to follow him when James out of nowhere, cried, 'Ben! THAT'S ENOUGH! COME BACK, EVERYTHING'S RE-VEALED…' Their trust in each other was so keen that Ben returned to the kitchen in complete admission of defeat upon hearing James' words.

…

'It's a sad end for Warel. I will need to go to the post to inform his family, may God help them. In any case, it's a good thing Ben and James did not try to oppose our suppression until the yard came to comprehend them. Good work boys… All right then, Mr Joy will manage the discharge operation until I am done with the yard's questioning and the post' were the captain's last words before he took off with the yard.

And so, the autumn's adventure was over. After a couple of days, I was discharged from my labour as a sailor for I had enough money in hand to manage a couple of months without regard to labour or money and focus on my aspiration. Thus, once discharged, I headed straight to London, where my lifetime's escapade began.'

…The End…'"

THE ADVENTURE OF
THE VENGEFUL ONE
SPRING II

And so we return to the present where the Land-lord has just finished narrating, 'The Incident that Occurred Last Autumn', in front of Williams and Mr Barnes. 'Sir, I'm speechless. Such a brilliant analysis!' remarked the Landlord as he returned the manuscript back to Williams.

'I merely used the rational part of my brain, nothing more. In which case, there you go, Mr Henderson. Now that you know last autumn's adventure, Jack, please proceed to what you have had in mind' replied Williams while returning to his armchair after placing the manuscript back on top of the pile of manuscripts.

'Indeed mate. Here ya go, read this article' replied Mr Barnes as he unfolded a piece of article, cut from the morning papers, more specifically the business section, taken from his coat, and handed it to Williams.

'Right. I will narrate the article for Mr Henderson to be on the same page with us. The article goes as so…

"New Houdini!?

British Imports and Exports in a state of Crisis!

"A ship being reported as missing is not a big deal… but is it? In the past 3 years, more than 200 cargo ships, owned by British businessmen, have been reported missing along with their crew-members. That number is more than 50 percent higher compared to the past decade! In fact, the ships have vanished into thin air! It is just as if the ocean casts a spell on the ship and once it sails, the ship vanishes into the ocean's hat. Until now, no one has any elucidation or enlightenment regarding the reason behind their disappearances. Many assumed at first that there was a manufacturing hindrance with the ships. But after distinguishing that there were many different manufacturers and different kinds of cargo ships, one thing was certain; a mysterious power is behind their disappearances.

"One thing nonetheless is certain regarding the business of their disappearances, which is that it has hurt the British economy massively! Foreign business owners neglect any import or export contracts that have a destination to or from the United Kingdom. Many are too petrified for their ships to disappear into thin air. This has been a massive hit to the British economy for the United Kingdom relies heavily on trade, more specifically, imports and exports. The decline in the demand for imports and exports with the United Kingdom is causing the British economy to undergo recession.

'Many English businessmen are travelling abroad to set up their businesses. No one is taking the risk of buying cargo ships, thus the ship's manufacturers are undergoing a demanding time business wise and financially. Will the vanishing of the ships create a new decade of global economic crisis and deflation? With the neglection of English business owners to buy cargo ships, unemployment rates have sky-rocketed! Social unrest is settling throughout sailors, engineers, officers, and cadets! The British Government still hasn't come up with an answer regarding the vanishing of those cargo ships. If they don't operate and come up with a solution, desperate measures may be taken by the British Parliament in order to restore back the British economy and global trading balance. Professor James Kane, British economist and a professor at the University of Harvard, anticipates that if no solution to regain the British imports' and exports' superiority and foreign businesses' confidence in the United Kingdom is made, the United Kingdom would, consequently, have to rely on desperate measures, such as the implementation of budget cuts, unemployment, benefits cuts, and public sector wages cuts, in the necessity of not only regaining the British economical balance but the global economic and trading balance-…'"

Williams halted reading for the rest of the article was chopped. Williams folded the article to its initial state and handed it back to Mr Barnes while taking a moment to reflect upon what he had just read. 'What do ya think mate?' asked Jack in eagerness. 'After reading this article, your words came back to me, and I used my rational train of thoughts. Why would such incidents take place?

The only rational conclusion I came up with was that there must have been someone pulling the strings from behind the scenes. Ain't that right Williams?'

'I will query you with a single question, Jack… Who do you think benefited from this bizarre business?' asked Williams while gazing at both his flat guests.

'I have reflected upon this question but couldn't come up with an answer. Who do you think?'

'I already know one side of the Benefiters' replied Williams with an intense expression. 'Initially, if we take our incident, for instance, we would see that the those who take off with ships may stand to profit. But it is irrational to think that 200 or more cargo ships were stolen by random criminals who had no contact with each other. Therefore, the next logical conclusion to assume is that there is a crime syndicate that provides those criminals, or in this case crew-members, to the cargo ships-…'

'Oh, I see. A shipping agency!' interrupted Mr Barnes with apprehension.

'Precisely! Upon investigation, and without much of a surprise, I uncovered a shipping agency which during the past three years kept expanding in power and profit while other shipping agencies, due to the crisis, went bankrupt. That was quite an obvious indicator for suspicion. The name of this shipping agency is "Blinders ltd". I have no doubt regarding its implications with the vanishing of the ships. It's not logical how such a company came into power at such a flying pace when it was only founded six years back. Without a doubt, they are one side of the Benefiters and crime syndicate.'

'By one side, you mean there are more Benefiters?' asked the Landlord.

'Indeed, my dear landlord! There are millions and millions of pounds in this game's implication. There must be a mastermind behind these blokes. Commanding and manipulating them with his strings!'

'I see… But what exactly is the plan here, Williams?' asked Mr Barnes in bewilderment.

'In the first place, it would be logical to infer that the ships and cargoes stolen are sold in the black market. We would need to investigate who is the person or organisation vending these two items in the black market. In the second place, we would need to investigate if Blinders ltd. is a British corporation founded by British Owners. If not, then we may have a long way to go.'

'How would we get access to the black market?'

'Don't fret over it. I have my source of information. I usually add a coded advertisement in the "Looking for employees" section of the evening or morning papers where, if you read the first letter of each word, you would come up with "COME JOY", which contains the clear meaning' answered Williams while trying to come up with an advertisement. 'In fact, here is what we would advertise today, 'Counsellor or marine engineer required to join on a yearlong contract.' Of course, determiners are excluded from the code, while other words might get excluded if required.'

'I see. Counsellor or Marine Engineer required to Join On a Yearlong contract. Quite ingenious, I must say', replied Mr Barnes in admiration.

'I wouldn't say so. Well, in any case, if we determined the first step, my dear Mr Henderson, would you do me this favour of advertising the code while Jack and I investigate the shipping agency?' asked Williams as he walked towards the settee to get a hold of his coat.

'With pleasure, sir!'

'Hold on… You mean, we're going to investigate the agency at this instance?'

'Precisely so, my dear Jack!' continued Williams, 'What are you waiting for? The complete annihilation of the British economy? Get going! By the time we get back here in the evening, our source with information will be here!' cried Williams as he rushed down the stairs.

…

In about three-quarters of an hour, Mr Barnes and Williams were standing in front of the Blinders ltd. building. 'Mate! How should we approach them?! We can't just walk inside casually!' whispered Mr Barnes as he saw Williams taking off and stepping inside the building. Instinctively, Mr Barnes followed Williams inside. While agonising over Williams' action, came Williams' reply in front of him, 'Just take my lead.' …

'Good afternoon sir, how may we help you?' asked the receptionist as they entered the building.

'Good afternoon. We have recently invested in a lady. We searched around for agencies and found ourselves here. Ain't that right, partner?' asked Williams of Mr Barnes, while turning with his gaze from the receptionist to him. Mr Barnes, taken suddenly by Williams, managed to agree with his apparently business partner. Williams, retaking controlling of the situation, asked the receptionist, 'We were told that you can help us hire crew-members?'

'Indeed, sir. Crew-members in what department precisely are you looking for?'

'We happen to be requiring a chief engineer and second and third officers', answered Williams, promptly with confidence.

'We can manage to find the right ones for you.'

'Do you happen to have a catalogue or a list with their resumes?' asked Williams with eagerness. This was the awaited moment he had longed for.

'We do have. One moment' replied the receptionist as he looked through the lists of employees, 'Here you go, sir.'

In Williams' hand at the moment were three documents with three different titles which were: 'Chief Engineers'', "Second Officers"', and "Third Officers"'. Williams took a couple of moments to go through the lists and arrived at the conclusion he desired. He proceeded to hand Mr Barnes the documents and asked the receptionist the employees' wages as to avoid creating any suspicions.

'Thanks, and greetings… oh one more issue. The agency appears well maintained. Do you happen to know the owner of the agency? We may decide to expand our business with him', asked Williams with the last thread of luck holding them from being suspected. Ordinarily, the owner of the ship would start to discuss the specifications of his ship and where exactly it is located. But at this point, Williams forgot the fact and committed a grave mistake which he hoped was just his superstition.

'I'm afraid sir we are not allowed to disclose any of our owners' or office employees' names without their permission', replied the receptionist without any moment to reflect upon the question which relieved Williams' restlessness.

'I understand', continued Williams, 'Cheers!' He strode outside the building while Mr Barnes followed him.

'Heavens, mate! What was that! I almost had a heart attack!' cried Mr Barnes once they left the building.

'Let's get some lunch. I happen to know a good cuisine around the corner. Once we go there, I will explain everything' replied Williams as he strode the street. Mr Barnes, naturally, strode along following him. Arriving at Williams' suggested place, they took their seats, ordered their food, and waited for their orders.

'Okay mate. The receptionist did not mention the names of the owners or any other information. What should we do next?' asked Mr Barnes in irritation while contemplating their current situation.

'The owners are British' came Williams' reply, full of confidence without a second of thought. Observing Mr Barnes' speechlessness, Williams proceeded to elucidate, 'I'm sure that you observed it but haven't thought about it. All the employees were British. There was not even one foreigner. It is a common tendency for business owners to bring along foreign employees from their respective country to make a profit for the employees' wages are usually lower than the natives. If our owner here was foreign, he would have had at least a couple of foreign employees for employment. But looking through at least 50 employees just now, there was not even one foreign employee to hire. Even local businessmen bring along foreign employees to make a profit, but not this agency. Suspicions must arise immediately if you think about this fact.'

'I see. Wait… If that is the fact, then Ben and James weren't related to neither the agency nor the crime syndicate for both of the lads were Irish', inferred Mr Barnes in realisation.

'Indeed. From what I remember, I think they got inspired by the vanishing of the ships tale and decided to impersonate the crime syndicates' acts. Unfortunately for them, the article they have read hadn't revealed how the ships vanished. In any case, here are our cuisines coming toward us. We will simply have to hear Benjy's information and decide our following course of action afterwards', replied Williams while fixing his whole attention towards their cuisines.

'Who is Benjy mate?' asked Mr Barnes, but all Williams cared about was the plate in front of him. Therefore, Mr Barnes' question passed from one of Williams' ear to the other unnoticed…

…

'Lucky man. I just happened to come across that information a couple of days ago', continued Benjy, apparently Williams' informant, who, once Mr Barnes came across his slim figure, sharp cheekbones and dark hair, Mr Barnes thought was a beggar leave aside an informant. 'The bulk cargo is apparently sold in 1000 pound sections with the exception of steel which depends on the type of steel. Unsurprisingly, all these cargoes are 90 percent sold from one organisation which is called 'vengeance-…''

Benjy was resuming his discussion, but for Williams, dark memories arose back in his mind. Memories which he hoped to forget but unfortunately couldn't. Uneasiness crept upon and grasped him by the neck. He had a hard time breathing. Sweat started to form on his forehead. 'Was it my imagination? Was I just confusing matters? Was I making a mistake?' thought Williams to himself when the voice of Benjy came to rescue him from his dark thoughts, 'Williams! Mate, I have to go. As always, if you need anything, make sure you advertise, and I will be sure to come' stated Benjy as he stretched his hand to receive his payment from Williams, which was more of a reward for him. 'Mr Barnes, it has been a pleasure meeting you sir. Now, if you'll excuse me.'

'Likewise', replied Mr Barnes as he observed Benjy's figure fading down the stairs. 'Accordingly, Williams, now that we know both sides of the Benefiters, what do you suggest is our course of action?' Williams, who still felt agitation grasping his neck, couldn't proceed on any course of action at the moment. He had to take his time to reflect upon this bizarre business. If what he had just recalled just now was correct, then it wouldn't be wise to keep Mr Barnes alongside me for his safety. 'Jack, my friend, I'm afraid I'm too weary to go on today. If it's convenient for you, would you like to give me a couple of days to reflect upon the matter?' A matter, thought Williams, which he might have to confirm in the gaols.

'Yeah, mate. No problem at all… I can observe your weariness. Just send me a post to this address or feel free to come by anytime you like in the next couple of days to "The Sailor's Inn". It seems like we will reconcile with our adventures once more!' suggested Mr Barnes while handing Williams a piece of paper with his address written upon it.

'I have heard about the inn. It is quite nearby actually. Perhaps a quarter of an hour's walk from here. No worries Jack, I will be sure to contact you!' replied Williams while embracing Mr Barnes and observing his figure, just as Benjy's, fading down the stairs…

Although Williams had not had any sleep since the past day when he woke up, there was no sign of sleepiness on his face. Instead, his face expressed one emotion which was concentration. Sitting on his armchair, facing the window, and gazing at his thoughts, Williams mind exploded with theories. Whether they were trivial or not, they just appeared to form in his mind. One thing was certain in his mind. The desire that his uneasy superstition was just his imagination. At this point, Williams had not realised, but the Landlord was knocking on his door. It wasn't until the Landlord raised his voice asking permission to enter Williams' flat that Williams' realised his presence, 'My apologies, Mr Henderson. Pray, come inside.'

'My sincere apologies sir, I know how weary you must be. I passed by the door earlier, but it just seems that I have missed this envelope which I observed just moments ago. It's for you.' Stated the Landlord as he approached Williams to hand him the envelope.

'No worries my dear', replied Williams. Williams waited for the Landlord to close the door behind him so that he could open the envelope, for it seemed that his reason of worry was indeed right… On the upper left side of the envelope, the letter 'V' was inscribed. A person whose name started with that letter Williams knew quite well. Opening the envelope and observing its contents, Williams' face grew so grotesque and furious that he was on the verge of punching through the window. The opening of the envelope disclosed an Inn card with the number '23' written below the inn's name. More specifically, it was a hotel card from "The Sailor's Inn". Williams deduced the number on the card was Mr Barnes room number. Williams knew full well the meaning behind this card. The crime syndicate they have been searching for have uncovered Mr Barnes' and Williams' involvement. Williams, in the span of one second, may have blamed himself a dozen times over his decision to involve his dear friend, Mr Barnes, in this grotesque business. 'If I just knew he was the one pulling the strings behind the scenes, I would've never accepted his involvement.' Williams reflected to himself.

Williams had no time to waste at this point. He had to reach Mr Barnes' inn as quickly as possible to check his safety. In reality, Williams did indeed waste no time. No second had passed since he glanced at the card and Williams remained in standing. In fact, At the moment he glanced at the card, Williams rushed towards the Inn without even wearing his coat when the temperature outside was chilling.

When he arrived at the inn, Williams took a deep breath as to prepare himself and strolled inside the building. He managed to arrive in front of the inn in less than seven minutes. William's running speed was equivalent to an Olympic runner. The adrenaline hormone which identifies us as human transformed Williams into another form of an advanced humanoid. Throughout the run, Williams only thought was concerning Mr Barnes' safety. 'Was the card just a threat? Was it a threat on my close ones? Was it a threat on my life?'…

Stepping inside the inn and towards the direction of Mr Barnes' room, Williams did not even hear the receptionist calling for him and asking if he required any help. Walking towards the room, Williams' uneasiness grew graver and graver. His field of vision blurred with shadows altogether except for the spot which indicated Mr Barnes' room number. Reaching the wanted room, Williams took another breath as to prepare himself, emotionally and physically, for what followed. Less than 10 minutes ago, Williams was in his flat, rethinking the case. Now, Williams, placing his right palm on Mr Barnes' hotel doorknob, opened the door with determination and preparation as to what awaited behind the door…

Darkness! 'The Room's lights seemed to be turned off which indicated the fact that either something grotesque occurred in the room, Jack is sleeping, or he has not arrived at the inn yet.' thought Williams to himself and wished for either of the latter two to be the reality. Customarily in hotels or inns, light switches were situated on the left wall as you enter a room. Therefore, Williams reached for the light switch with his left arm in order to turn on the lights. As Williams reached for the light switch, his arm trembled with fear and worry. An eternity passed in the span of a second. He chose to leave this world rather than find which one of his three theories was the reality once he opens the light switch.

After an eternity of adonization, Williams' left arm finally managed to find the light switch. The instance Williams switched on the lights that enlightened the room, Williams glanced throughout the room, observing everything. The moment Williams glanced at what was inside the room, a second worth of time in the living world passed, but for Williams, it felt like years. A second where he questioned reality. Whether what was occurring at the moment was reality? Whether he had made a mistake? Whether it was a mistake taking Mr Barnes to the agency with him? Was that exact moment a reality? Williams, a private investigator in London, standing in front of an inn's room, was it a reality? The reason Williams' 'second' took years was for, inside the room, on the ground in front of the door, lay the body, which Williams' assumed a corpse for there was a wound on the centre of its forehead, of his dear friend, Mr Jack Barnes.

...

With the termination of Williams' second, he rushed to his friend's corpse to see if there was an ounce of life in his friend's body. After checking the pulse various times on his friend's neck and wrists, Williams, out of desperation, tried various futile attempt to bring life back to him. Facing reality, Williams realised that on his friend's chest, a folded piece of paper was placed. Clearly, without much of a thought, Williams knew from whom the paper was. Following the comprehension of the letter addressed to him, Williams swore upon himself to bring justice upon the letter's author. His purpose was now to terminate the crime syndicate and the mastermind behind it. An objective that could potentially end Williams' life in the process, regrettably, in vain. The letter which caused Williams to act this was the following;

"If thee frolic in the vicinity of fire, fire shall scald thee,

Upon my game, thee accepted audaciously,

Thence, in these wise words, thee are bound to agree,

'All is fair in love, war, and rivalry.'

-Richard Vandican"

Folding the paper back to its initial observed state, Williams walked towards the bedsheet he had observed in front of him. Holding the bed sheet in his arms in agony, regret, desperation, and most notably determination, Williams, while taking a good and final look upon his dear friend's face as a final goodbye, placed it upon Mr Jack Barnes' motionless, yet blooming in Williams' mind, corpse…

…The End…

THE ADVENTURE OF THE BLEEDING HEART

WINTER I

It's rather seldom to witness such an unclouded day in London', marveled Williams Joy, a young Holmesian whose goal is to write a monograph on the late Mr Sherlock Holmes, the greatest mind in England. Or perhaps the whole world, that's how Williams and many more regarded him, detective methods. 'Aha! And here's our robin', exclaimed Williams as he bent down looking through the window at the postman walking towards the lodge. A few moments, perhaps minutes, went by when the Landlord bashed the door, 'Landlord sir, it's the daily morning mail', stated the Landlord.

'Pray, my dear Landlord, come in and take a seat', answered Williams.

'I haven't seen weather akin to today', said the Land-lord while handing Williams his letters, 'since me

days in the countryside as a child. Such sinless days.'

'Indeed. Quite hard to leave such weather unnoticed', replied Williams while going through his letters.

'Anything peculiar sir? Instead of the accustomed bills and taxes?' asked the Landlord as he noticed Williams observing a letter in his hands rather unusually.

'ye…' answered Williams unconsciously while taking this few and far between letter from its envelope.

'yes sir?' Williams paused a couple of moments before answering back. He took his time to read off the load of papers. Indeed, and what a load. Who would send off perchance like 15 pages folded together so that they fit in the tiny envelope? 'People nowadays,' thought Williams to himself 'grinding a manuscript in an envelope half its size to conserve fees.' 'A letter indeed, my dear, or more precisely, a STORY!' exclaimed Williams.

'A sto-story sir? May I…'

'I know its perplexing to comprehend, that's the mo-tive why I want you, my dear Landlord, to narrate this story audibly. Might be your chance to realise more about this peculiar letter, or perhaps this manuscript.'

'Wel… With pleasure, sir. Why shan't I?' replied the Landlord with the old-fashioned British eagerness as he stretched his hand to take hold of the bundle of papers.

'Excellent!' cried Williams with a thrill as he seated himself on his armchair and closed his eyelids for a full attentiveness on the following narration.

Winter. Christmas and winter. People seem to connect them both. Some argue that winter is pointless without Christmas. Seems a fair argument. At least in Britain it always is. The Christmas spirit, or perhaps, the winter spirit. Where every family gathers with one another, individuals who may have never seen each other for perhaps dozens of years may gather with one another on this day, Christmas eve. Where every family has made its plans months before. Every family! Maybe not, at least this young married couple didn't. Still five days to go and negative arrangements are formed.

'Charles, who's this Mary girl you've been talking to. If you're planning on leaving me, just know I'll poison you before you do it first old boy. I've been reading detective novels, you know.' cried Mrs. Abby Charles full of wrath.

'Delusional as always. Give me a rest, will ya Abby?' replied Mr Charles.

'If you want some rest then go spend this Christmas with that ratbag Mary of yours.'

'Indeed, indeed. Will go', answered Charles without giving awareness to her accusations.

'In any case, Charles darling, we need to arrange our plans for Christmas. I assume we have no time left anyways' cried Abby with slight optimism for her aching to be satisfied.

'What's wrong with staying in our warm home. No good wasting money on fancy hotels and expensive wine for just one day. Besides, we still have the new year to go', replied Charles, shattering her dreams with his everyday gay attitude.

'Always like this. All you care about is your work. I bet you honey, if work manifested itself into a body, I would be still living with my mother. God bless her, always accepting me', cried Abby with sarcasm looking through the window at the white covering the streets.

'Mentioning your mother, I contemplate she invited us to spend those couple of Christmas days with her', stated Charles as he held a letter in his hands.

'What's that you're saying?'

'Nothing, just that your prayers were answered.'

'You mean we have plans for Christmas?' asked Abby full of hope and joy.

'Uhh-yes... your mother invited us to spend those couple of days with her.'

'Oh, really darling, and when will we leave to my dear mother?'

'Plausibly we shall leave by tomorrow's morning train.'

'Well then, I will hurry up and prepare our bags', declared Abby as she strode to their bedroom.

...

The next morning the married couple were on their way to Abby's mother, who lives in the countryside with 10-minutes till their destination. 'I hope you didn't forget any of your important belongings' said Charles, mocking Abby.

'Men don't have a clue about how important it is for a woman to have a specific item for every occasion.

Look at yourselves, just pigs wearing the same garments for every occasion there is!' cried Abby with anger.

'Yeah, darling, sure thing. We are the pigs. As you say.' As they argued, time passed by without them noticing until they eventually reached their destination. 'Halle-lujah! At last, we're here', cried Abby while getting out of the car and watching the sight in front of her; her old house. Many years have passed since she viewed this house.

And what a house! Her family wasn't what they would call nowadays 'well-heeled', but her father was a virtuoso in economics... 'Will go knock on the door', cried Abby as she went to the door. Charles was removing the bags out of the car and following her 'Women, why do they need these many bags. Hell, if I know! And why would she ever bring her tennis racquet with her. Good lord! take me to the devil!' murmured Charles to himself. The door opened to the dark-haired maid standing behind it. 'Mrs. Charles! Been a while since I have last seen you. Your mother is so anxious to see you. Ms Ann too', exclaimed the maid with enthusiasm.

'Lisa! How's it been, my girl? Indeed, been a while. How's mother? I hope she stopped smoking those small cigarettes of hers. Not good for her health. And how's Ann? Oh little Ann. Been dying to see her', said Abby as she strolled to the living-room, guided by the maid while poor Charles, was left behind with the bags. "Should have foreseen this was going to happen", he murmured to himself.

They waited in a living-room that was perhaps as big as their entire apartment back in London. A few moments went by when a voice came coming down the stairs, 'Abby! My dear little girl, how have you been these past years? I see your man is here. How was handling my girl, dear old Charles? I hope she doesn't cause you any hitches' cried the mother as she hugged the two mature grownups that were now more like school brats in front of her.

'Dear mommy, we've been fine. I just can't stop feeling that one day he would run off away from me with another woman, but other than that we've been doing fine. What about you, dear? How's everything? Pretty sure it's boring down here. I thank the Lord for getting me out of here. Where's Ann?'

'Whose calling my name without my authority? Oh, it's just dear old Abby. Still revolting since you've left us', said Ann coming behind her mother from down the stairs.

'We used to fight because of this attitude of yours,' replied Abby, with slight annoyance.

'I don't know what good you've spotted in her, Charles. Should have married a normal one.'

'Now that's as far as...' Abby started shouting when the mother stopped her, 'Alright my girls, that's enough. I'm sure you're quite tired driving all the way here. We don't need to show you upstairs, do we, Abby?

You weren't gone for that long,' said the mother with laughter.

'No mother, you don't. Perhaps we will get some rest. Charles?' asked Abby, looking eagerly at Charles.

'Indeed. I'm pretty tired driving all the way here', answered Charles while following Abby upstairs with

the bags.

'Make sure to wake up for dinner. It's at five', cried the mother behind them.

Abby strolled the stairs and turned to her right to face a long corridor with doors. That's where members of the family stay, but I reason we should stay in the guest rooms for my room would be too small for us both.

'Or I would've slept on the floor and you, the tyrant you were, would've slept on the bed', remarked Charles as he followed Abby turning left and walking to the guest rooms.

...

Abby and Charles woke up at a quarter of an hour to five. 'Charles! Charles! Wake up we're late!' cried Abby, while she hustled up and prepared herself.

'No, I'm not late, I'm just going to wear my garments, you're a long way to go if you're willin' to use the chemicals on your face', replied Charles half-awake on the bed.

'They're no chemicals! And get out of the bed and buzz up this dress's Zip on my back that I can't reach!'

'Okay... Okay'

Ten minutes later they were strolling down the stairs. "We did it in time", murmured Abby to herself. They walked towards the table where everyone was waiting for them, but it seems that they weren't the only guests. Three new guests were at the table. The first one Abby spotted was a woman of middle age, possibly older than twenty-five and most assuredly younger than thirty. She was wearing a blue dress that fitted her accordingly. She had had straight black hair that matched her eyes and was the opposite of her snowy skin. She was "hella pretty" as Charles would say. The other, she observed, was possibly her mother. She had the same facial features as the young lady but was older obviously. She was wearing the same coloured dress as her possible daughter with the same black hair and eyes.

Lastly, she perceived a young man. She couldn't put his height for he was resting but, she thought he was neither too tall nor short, maybe 6 feet. From his garments, it was evident to assume that he was quite a muscular young man who's well dressed and knew his suits. Women call these young men nowadays, 'gentlemen'. 'Women, giving everything a name nowadays', Abby remembered Charles' saying. Nevertheless, the young man had short hair and brown eyes with tanned skin.

'Any young lady would fall for him', thought Abby to herself.

'Hello mother, glad we weren't too late. I see we have guests this Christmas' remarked Abby to her mother.

'Indeed, we have! This is my daughter Abby and her husband, Mr Charles. Abby, Charles, this is Ms Ruth and her mother Mrs Claude. Ruth was friends with your sister in her late years of education. The young gentleman is Mr Williams Joy. He helped your late father in an implication he faced, and we thought we might as well invite him this Christmas', replied the mother while gesturing with her hands towards them.

'I hope you will enjoy your Christmas time here in our modest house', said Abby as she walked towards her seat.

'I'm sure we will', replied Ruth with enthusiasm. Dinner was eaten and complete at about half-past five. All the house member gathered in the living-room afterwards for the old-fashioned tea time. 'I see your garden is wholly well maintained. Quite stunning too. Do you have a Gardner?' asked Mrs Claude, looking through the window.

'My late husband used to take care of the garden. He took care of it as if it was his own son. After his death, we thought we might bring in a Gardner twice a week to maintain it', replied the mother.

'You used to maintain it as well mother. Well, perhaps you've aged', uttered Abby

'Quite so, my dear, quite so.'

'Ruth, my dear, tell me, what path did you choose to take? I hope you've found a well paid decent job', said Ann turning her head to face Ruth.

'I've found one. And a good one too. Fortunately, some business proprietor was looking for a secretary and a friend of mine working there recommended me. Four hundred pounds a year. Quite a decent salary for a woman to earn this much', replied Ruth with joy.

'I'm happy for you, my dear.'

'What about you, Ann?' asked Ruth.

'Helping my mother with the orthodox family business. I hope I will get all the experience I can from her in these coming years.'

'I perceive, I perceive…'

'What about you, my dear Williams? How's your Sherlockian adventure been going?' asked the mother.

'Sherlockian!' exclaimed Charles.

'Indeed Sherlockian. He's a detective! A consultant as luck would have it, inspired by the greatest of his time, Sherlock Holmes!' replied the mother.

'I see, well if you're really inspired, what do you see?' asked Charles eagerly.

'Oh, Charles don't interrogate him. He's a guest. Remember!' said Abby flushed with embarrassment.

'No, no, no, no. Why not mademoiselle? It would be my utmost contentment', cried Williams with a slight beam on his face that showed his confidence.

'Very well. What do you see Mr Holmes junior?'

'Let us start by saying your occupation. It's very likely that your occupation is a medical practitioner, more precisely a surgeon. An eye surgeon. One of your hobbies is reading, you have been to France, and you used to

pla…'

You've got me, you've got me. You win. Perhaps it wouldn't bother you telling us your reasoning?' interrupted Charles.

'Certainly not. Let's see. You're an eye surgeon for I see a scratch on your hand that would only be inflicted by one of your surgery tools used in an eye surgery. I believe they are called spring forceps. When we shook hands, you didn't embrace mine. This is a typical attitude for surgeons who consider their fingers their most precious possession unlike an archetypal Londoner, who grasps your hands during a handshake. I observed you wearing your pince-nez a couple of times, but you weren't reading. Your way of wearing it is used very classically to help while you're reading. This shows how reading persuaded you to adopt this way of wearing the pince-nez for a long time. Lastly, your chemise's button is from France. I know the branding for I've been there', elucidated Williams lastly while taking a deep sigh after he finished.

'I concede, I'm impressed. It all looks so simple now being elucidated, but you're missing two points', claimed Charles.

'Which are?'

'Firstly, I'm an orthopaedic surgeon. I admit you had a good guess based on the spring forceps but, they're also used for other surgeries apart from the eye. Secondly, how is it that you know I'm a Londoner?' asked Charles eagerly while bending his back to get closer to Williams.

'Oh, should've known that. Damn goddess of ratiocination, why did you fail me! Anyhow, elementary!

Your accent gave you away, not to mention you're wearing a pair of boots that can only be custom-made in London', answered Williams with a sigh.

'So unfussy', murmured Charles, 'simple and magnificent!'

'Eyes and brains, as Mr Holmes would say, "eyes and brains".'

'Oh dear, you're fantastic! I wish I had a brain like yours', exclaimed Ann with admiration.

'Don't get your hopes up, little sister. You're no way reaching his intellectualism.'

'Stop it, girls. Don't start fighting now', interrupted the mother. And so, half an hour or so later each went to his and her own rooms. Tired they may be, they can relax now. 'Where are you going now, dear? Aren't we gonna rest a little?' asked Abby to her husband who seemed to be preparing to go out.

'Will go for a walk in the countryside. Quite rare for me to visit this place', answered Charles with his back to her.

'Will come with you then.'

'No, I don't think it's a good idea. Better stay here with your mother and sister. You didn't see them for quite a while. Better take advantage of this situation and spend as much time with them as possible', said Charles as he opened the door and left.

'Yes, I think you're rig... wai...' murmured Abby when she looked through the window and saw a figure standing beside the house. 'I think that's Ruth. What's she doing there... Charles? What's he doing? Why is he walking towards her? Why are they strolling along with each other on the sideway? How come Charles knows

143

this random girl?" Abby started murmuring to herself as she watched their silhouettes vanish away from her sight. Abby, in that same spot, anxious, dissatisfied, more importantly, hurt. Maybe she was too hasty to judge the situation? 'I'm sure there must be a reason…', she started whispering to herself, making out excuses for Charles. 'It's always been like this', she thought 'always with a young girl. Am I getting old now and I'm no more of use to him? But surely, ever since we've married, he always chit-chatted with some woman. Every time I face him with it, he rebuttals by saying, "It's nothing. Just a chit chat. Am I not allowed to talk to women anymore?" well now I have evidence. The Evidence of my own eyes!'

As she thought those last few words, the door opened, and he was back. Charles, as gay as always didn't mind if his wife, Abby, would've seen him. Just acted on his own. 'Where have you been?' asked Abby with slight anger.

'Surely darling, I've tol…' 'You didn't tell me about strolling on the street side with this Ruth girl. How come you know her? Who is she?' interrupted Abby, full of anger.

'Oh, she. Don't mind her. She's an old acquaintance of mine. I just didn't see her for a while and wasn't expecting to come across her here. So, I told myself to go and see how's she doing', answered Charles with his usual calm, gay attitude. Abby's anger seemed to degrade. It certainly did. 'I think he's telling the truth. Why wouldn't he be? I think it's reasonable why he's done what he did', thought Abby to herself. Was she too credible? Too blunt? Too candid? Who knows, maybe she is just rational. 'I'm… I'm sorry, Charles. Should have asked you calmly. I'm just… it's just…'

'Don't worry about it. I'm used to this. Don't mind yourself with it. Let's just rest for the day and go to bed', said Charles as he approached her and slid his arm around her waist.

'Dear darling Charles', murmured Abby while falling asleep.

Three Days till Christmas Eve

Dreams, a whole world made from our sub-conscious. For some, it's as real as their logic. For others, just an illusion or perhaps a hallucination. The next morning Abby had woken up with a jolt. 'What was this dream!' she murmured to herself. 'Just- just a bad dream... I should get back to sleep. It's too early. Even Char... Charles? Where is he? Why would Charles get up so early?... Maybe it wasn't just a dream, after all. Dreaming about him. HIM LEAVING ME! Will it happen? Is Charles having an affair? I bet he is with that good for nothing woman.' Abby got up, walked to and fro the room. Thinking to herself. Worrying herself. Blaming herself. Why would he do such a thing? 'Am I not fulfilling his longings? Am I... am I?' she thought to herself. 'This weather... White. Sinless. Pure. Is... is that Charles! What is he doing? Why... why is his hand on that woman's neck? Why is he looking at her like this? B... but he told me she's just an old acquaintance. Did he... did he make up a whopper? Why would he?... I'm worrying myself for no reason. I'm sure there must be a rational explanation. I'm sure... I'm sure...' and so thought Abby to herself as she went to the bathroom and prepared for breakfast.

An hour later, she was seated on the breakfast table, holding a spoon and making a strawberry jam sandwich. 'Hello there, sloppy head. Slept well tonight?' asked Ann coming down the stairs.

'Just woken up from a bad dream. Maybe I should stop taking this damned sleeping draught after all', replied Abby as she took a bite of the sandwich.

'A nightmare? At least you're dreaming about something. I fall asleep and wake up at the same time.'

'Humans… Such weird creatures…', murmured Abby.

…

'Isn't that Mr Williams? Perhaps I shall go up to him and give him some circle. Seems lonely', murmured Abby to herself while going towards Williams who was sitting in the garden. 'Good afternoon Mr Williams. Quite nice weather for this year's Christmas.'

'Good afternoon to you too mademoiselle. Indeed we should take advantage of this weather. Quite seldom', replied Williams while looking upward, towards the sky.

'We shall thank the lord for this weather. Always merciful.' Replied Abby as she followed Williams's gaze towards the sky.

'Possibly possibly.'

'Speaking of our lord. What church do you go to, Mr Williams?' asked Abby while looking at Williams eagerly. There was a pause. Williams turned his head towards her then looked at the ground and gave a sigh 'Not a devotee to religions.'

'Quite unreligious, aren't you. Most young men are like you nowadays. They forget about their lord and go living their lives. I'm not speaking of you, of course, dear.'

'No mademoiselle. Don't get me wrong. I am a logician. A rationalist. Logic is my tool for living. I use my eyes and brains to guide me. Ratiocination is my weapon. Please, rather mind chewing over this topic. I hope you understood my meaning', Abby paused. She stared at Williams for a while. Trying to figure out what his exact meaning was when it flashed her mind, 'is this young man in his sane abilities? Is he really suggesting that he's an infidel?' she thought, 'people like him fright me. I shall, perhaps go.' She got up, 'Was good having a tête-à-tête with you, Mr Williams. I think I'm gonna go now and wrap my tennis racquet's handle with the free time I've on my hands', and went to her room.

...

'Who's calling me? What's this voice?' Abby asked herself unconsciously. She didn't realise that she was still in her deep world, and Charles was trying to grip her from it. 'Abby! Abby! We're gonna be late for dinner. Get up.'

'Yes, yes coming', replied Abby as she came to full consciousness now, 'Give me 10 minutes and I'll be ready.' As per her word, both were seated at the dinner table after a quarter of an hour.

'You're always the last to arrive honey. Be more step-by-step', pointed out the mother.

'Yes mother, will do', replied Abby as she took her seat. Dinner was eaten, and as per folklore, tea was served afterwards in the living-room where everyone was gathered. 'The food was one of a kind. I'm lost for words', exclaimed Mrs Claude.

'I know my dear. My husband brought the chef with him when he came back from South Africa. He told us we would love his food, and just like he had said, we are in submission with it', replied the mother.

'I quite agree. His cuisine was quite impressive. The food melts in your mouth', exclaimed Williams. And so, tea time was spend discussing cuisine styles and different kinds of food from around the globe. At approximately a quarter past seven, everyone went to their rooms. And yet again, like a wicked dream a dire déjà vu. 'Charles? Are you going to stroll the streets again?' asked Abby as she observed Charles holding his black coat.

'Indeed, little girl. Walking is a good exercise after a heavy meal', replied Charles preparing to depart.

'Are you going to meet this Ruth woman again?'

'No... Uhh... Y-yes... Why are you asking?'

'Why am I asking! I think I know what's going on. You're willing to leave me for her. I know you. I know these doctors' tricks. You're planning to make me take an overdose of sleeping draught so I can set you free! I know! I know! Why don't you just tell me the truth,' cried Abby at Charles with anger.

'What are you bluffing about? Are you nuts? Just- just behave your...'

'Behave myself! You're a liar. I know that. I've seen you with dozens of other girls before, and you're trying to tell me you didn't have any kind of affair with neither of those women. Please!'

'Abby, my dear. Please stay calm', said Charles walking towards her. 'Everything's going to be okay. It's just a chit chat, you know. Nothing more, nothing less. I was the surgeon who made the surgery for her father. Don't worry girl. I'm gonna go now. Relax for the day and spend it with your mother', said Charles as he sported his coat and prepared to leave.

'Everything's gonna be okay? Everything's gonna be okay? Everything's gonna be okay? N-no...' thought Abby to herself...

'Okay Charles darling. Its cold outside, so don't stroll for long. I'll go to mother and spend some time with her.'

...

'Mother! Old pussy, don't worry, will be fine', said Abby while she was getting up to return to her bedroom. 'Will go back now to get some rest.'

'Abby y…' Ann started saying when her mother inter-rupted, 'It's up to scratch.'

Abby walked across the corridor. She totally forgot now about Charles and his mischiefs. Everything was well-honed now. She sauntered slowly—five more steps till her room. The lights were dim. Something, she felt, was peculiar. She came at last at her door. She stood there, stood silently. She felt something off beam, but she hushed the feeling away. She began opening the door 'What's this! she murmured, 'Why is everything so cha-otic. Everything's upside down'. She opened the door fully and walked inside the chaotic room where drawers were opened, bags searched to their core, and as if a gale hit this room. 'It's freezing here. Have I left the window open? Why did I…' she thought 'what's that?' she cried as she tripped on something. 'Its-it's a body!' Her heart sank at the sight of this body. The curtain on her eyes started to unveil to her surroundings—a body with its face facing the floor. Possibly dead for it seems it has multiple blows on the back of its head. Multiple blows? More like a dozen!

She looked around, and now it came to her, 'BLOOD!' Blood was everywhere around the room. Pond of blood beneath the body. Blood. This much blood can come off from a body? Who would murder someone like this? The back of the body's skull was disfigured. Abby looked at the body and noticed something! 'I know this coat!' she thought, 'It-it can't be!' While thinking, she bent down to the body and twisted it when it struck her, 'Charles! Oh no Charles! It can't be! Who would do such a thing to Charles! Charles! CHARLES! Someone! Please come and help!'

Help my dear Charles, please! somebody!" shouted and screamed Abby at the top of her throat. She shouted and shouted. She wasn't mindful of her actions. Tears started to fall. Tear after tear. Time passed like hours. She was in a world of despair. Her heart, she thought, stopped beating. Skipped a beat. This moment. It was Despair. Sorrow. Grief. Her dear Charles, now gone. Never coming back. Who would do such a thing? Who... 'GET AWAY FROM THE CORPSE, IMME-DIATELY!' yelled a voice in the back. Abby raised her head and looked at the figure standing at the door. She couldn't focus her vision for her tears were in the way. 'DID YOU HEAR ME YOU FOOL? GET AWAY FROM THE BODY! YOU'LL TAMPER WITH THE EVIDENCE!' At those mere words, Abby came to her full consciousness. 'Mr Williams. I-I- What occurred? Is Charles-Is Charles dead?' Members of the household began gathering outside the room, murmuring to each other and asking questions. Williams, who was the expert at this moment and more importantly, the man, started taking authority of the situation. 'Mademoiselle, please get out of the room. Now! Madam Ann, give her a cup of brandy. It will do her good. Madam Ruth, go and call the country police and the inspector.'

As per his orders, Abby got out of the room and went with her sister, who was trying to tranquil her 'Now, now, little girl. Stay calm and stop sobbing', she said.

'Now that everything's composed. I can investigate. I hope she didn't tamper that much with the evidence' thought Williams to himself. He walked inside the room and noticed its anarchy. He looked at the window, and immediately a thought flashed through his brain, 'a possible burglary attempt?' He bent to the body and tried its pulse, 'no good, dead from an hour. What's this! Dozen blows to the back of the head? Heavy blows. What's the weapon? It seems like he had been struck with something similar to a heavy stick. It must be here some-

where. A burglar wouldn't prefer to keep it in his pocket'
He thought, as he looked around the room.

'AHA! The tennis racquets! That's the weapon. This is
some grotesque business I'm dealing with. The room is
full of blood. Walls, bed, floor, desk, and window. Everything has blood. Burglary attempt and murder? I need to
investi…'

'Called the police, sir', said Ruth while standing outside
the room.

'Excellent. But they're no good. I think I've solved this
murder.'

'Did you- you know who murdered Mr Charles in such
a grotesque manner, sir?'

'Possibly, I need to investigate more.'

…

'Abby, darling. Drink this brandy. It will do you good',
said Ann as she attempted to force the brandy down Abby's throat.

'Charles! Charles! I can't believe it. I can't. My dear
Charles!' cried Abby with tears falling.

'Here you go, little girl. Everything's gonna be okay.
Don't worry. Charles's in a better place now', said the
mother to calm her down.

'My dear Charles…'

…

A tragedy. That's the word for a situation such as this
one. And what a tragedy. One that is filled with blood.
A room full of bleeding hearts. The beloved husband
dead. Who would attempt a burglary at such a time of
the year?

Damn those burglars. Bringing despair everywhere behind them. Such a nice family is filled with anguish now. Everything broken down into pores. Into bleeding hearts. But for Williams, it was ecstasy. Heaven! He thought he would have perished from world-weariness. Now he shall satisfy himself. But what was he saying? He came across the sinner? Perhaps he wouldn't name it a sin for his logicality, but it's not the case for now. How come he came across the sinner? Were there fingerprints that would bring him to justice? In that case, it makes sense. Or else?... Or else?

...

An hour later, Williams gathered all the household members in the living-room to discuss the situation. The police notified the household that it would take at least an hour or so for the yard to arrive. Murder is not the country's speciality; hence they must call up the experts. In the meanwhile, Williams took authority of the situation

'Madams. Mademoiselles. Once we discuss this situation, I'm sure we would arrive at a right and proper deed', he declared.

'What deed are you talking about?' asked the mother.

'I have come across the murderer. The cause of despair.'

'What do you mean Mr Williams? Isn't it a burglary attempt? We need to find the burglar', cried Ann.

'Madam. I can assure you this is by no means a burglary attempt.'

'What do you mean? Who else would mess around a room in such a chaotic manner? It must be a burglar.

There is no other person capable of doing so.'

'Have you though...'

'What about the ladder? Who would position a ladder beside the window with the omission of a burglar?'

'Madam. Please control yourself.'

'Ann. Let us hear what he's got to say', said the mother with authority.

'Thank you, mademoiselle. Now ladies. I've investigated every part of the house and thought of everything and eliminated all the useless facts with the omission of the important. Let me start by the following. When I first walked through the room, I neither saw chaos nor burglary. What I saw was hatred. A burglar would never murder a person in a situation where the burglar can't afford to murder one. The body was hit dozens of times on the back of the head with a tennis racquet. Anyhow, I searched through the room, and excuse me mademoiselle Abby, but I had to search through your belongings so that I could make sure that it wasn't a burglary, and what puzzled me is that a box with jewellery was on the top of the drawer where he, the theoretical burglar, had supposedly searched and didn't attempt to yield. A burglar would conventionally know that in this situation he's in a pot full of gold. Why did he continue to search? A normal burglary then was immediately eliminated from my mind.

'The next possibility I thought about was a planned burglary. Could it be that a burglar was searching for? something in the first place? Did he find what was he searching for? The possibility is low for he wouldn't have murdered Monsieur Charles. Hence, the thing he's searching for must be still in the room but again, why would he murder the victim with such abhorrence? Such hatred? I kept this possibility aside for a while.

'Another possibility is that all of the above was a fabrication. Could it be that it was murder disguised as burglary? If so, the only dilemma is that the deed doer must have been a member of the household!'

'Mr Williams! Please don't say such nonsense!' cried the mother.

'Mother. Let us see what he's got to say.'

'Let's eliminate the case of burglary from out-of-doors for the moment. The first notion that came to me was that Ms Ruth and her mother planned the burglary.'

'Monsieur Williams ple…', cried the mother but Williams interrupted her 'Mademoiselle, please let me finish. As per saying, I thought that perhaps madam Ruth was deliberately taking M. Charles out of the room so that her mother would search the room freely. I admit, I was convinced by this notion when certain factors changed my train of thought: 1- The blow was a heavy one. Mrs Claude would not be able to deliver such a blow. 2- The blow was from the back. Which means that he was murdered by a close associate. Someone that he had trusted to give his back to. Certainly, if M. Charles noticed Mrs Claude lurking in his room, he wouldn't turn his back to her so that she would strike him from behind. Except… except if Ruth caught sight of her mother when she was standing behind M. Charles when he opened his room's door and had to think of something swiftly.

'But the body…'

'Yes… Was found with its head pointing towards the door. I thought it was a possibility for them to turn the body 180 degrees calculatingly to misguide us; hence I kept that in my mind. 3- The tennis racquet came from inside the room. Mademoiselle Abby informed me about her racquet and how she was willing to wrap its handle.

Hence, the second point I mentioned was now a low likelihood.'

'She's the one! Isn't she! I saw her! I saw her talking with Charles and going on walks with him!' cried Abby. 'You took my dear Charles away from me because you couldn't have him! I saw him resting his hand on your throat! He wasn't giving up on me, so you had to take him!'

'There you go Abby. Behave', said her sister.

'It's understandable that she's behaving the way she is. There was nothing between Mr Charles and myself' Ruth started saying, 'He certainly had his hand on my throat. After all, he was the surgeon who mended my throat. He's an orthopaedic surgeon after all.'

'But I thought, but I thou…'

'You thought your husband was having an affair?' said Williams, 'Ultimately, my dear ladies, I come to this in-ference. When I look at the psychology of this crime. Of its attempt for fabrication. Of its abhorrence. It all flashed through my mind that the only one who could've murdered your husband and take him away from you is only yourself, mademoiselle Abby!

…

'What! What are you talking about Mr Williams? Sure-ly, you're mistaken. I left- I left Charles alive and went to my mother. I'm sure. I didn't kill my-my Charles my-my beloved.'

'Mademoiselle. A blind man will see the sudden hatred in this crime. From the moment you arrived here, I pre-sumed something about you. I presumed that you are a possible schizophrenic. Isn't she Madam Ann? Certain evidence displayed this. How you alleged most of your husband's exploits. The way you spoke with him. Always sensing that he's having an affair. Always mistrusting him. Believing he might one day poison you for another woman.'

'No- no I didn't! I didn't do it!'

'And then, perhaps, as you say. You saw Ruth waiting for your husband downstairs. You couldn't take it. He turned his back and walked away. You felt he might never come back to you after this. You saw him vanishing away. You grabbed the racquet you told me about and what had occurred afterwards was shown upstairs. The abhorrence. The hatred. The envy. The emotion. An emotional wrongdoing. By your reaction now, I believe you could not remember what had occurred at the time of the tragedy. I assumed there might be a possibility of this happening. The trauma. The blood. The trauma, I perhaps reason, triggered you to have what they call Psychogenic Amnesia, causing you to disremember what occurred and act as if everything is normal. An erased memory. When you walked to your mother's room, I remember you speaking to someone inside, yes. You were speaking to your husband. Informing him you're leaving or something between those lines. But mademoiselle, he was already dead at that moment. I'm sorry if I'm being forthright with you, but I only care about the truth.'

'No. NO! I didn't murder him. I can't believe such a thing I can't I ca…' That's when everything flashed like lightning to Abby—watching Charles walking away. Vanishing into thin air. Having her vision on the racquet near her. Holding it. 'NO! I DIDN'T!' Getting closer and closer to Charles when, 'NO IT CAN'T! CHARLES!' Abby screaming, shouting, as her memories came back. Holding her head, tears of waterfalls, sitting on the ground.

Her memories… "YOU WILL NOT LEAVE ME" the body striking the floor. Charles, his face, on the floor. Abby, bending on the floor, hammering, thumping, and hitting Charles. Has she realised what had she had done? Striking with full power. On Charles. She isn't influencing herself. It's the power of love, but isn't love supposed to be all about contentment? Why is she so wounded? "LOVE" what did it mean to be in love? Was Abby in love? If so, why was she so hurt? So hurt she feels her heart's bleeding. Hurt. Wounded. Abby, remembering the blood. Blood on her face. On her garments. On her hands. A bleeding heart inside out.

'Abby my dear, it's gonna be okay. How can you say such a thing, Mr Williams, without any evidence! I'm sure, anyone would have noticed her if she was worn in blood', cried Ann as she held her sister around her arms.

'Yes, madam. That's why I said it was a fabrication. And I'm sure you know what I'm hinting about.' There was a pause. Complete silence now. No one minded Abby's screaming. Everyone looking at Williams. No one knew what he meant. Perhaps she knew? Fabrication? What does he mean?

'How come you know' Started the mother asking and breaking the silence 'About what we have done?'

'As I've mentioned. Certain factors changed my train of thought. One of them was Ms Ann saying, 'If it wasn't a burglary, then how come there's a ladder beside the window.' Madam, how come you know of the ladder if you've stayed with your sister all the time and could not have possibly known about or seen the ladder.' Silence. Closed souls. It came to light now. Ann and her mother fabricating the evidence. Making the room look as if there had been a burglary. Trying to save their family. Saving Abby. Abby, in despair, in tears! In sorrow! Mourn! How could she have executed her own soulmate? Her most beloved one. Abby, with a bleeding heart. Abby, in such pain no one can understand. Her heart, she feels, might burst out of her chest. She can't take this feeling anymore!

She would rather go to him. To apologise. But will he accept her apology? 'Dear old Charles.'

There was a knock on the door, and it seemed that it was the yard. 'Don't worry,' said Williams abruptly, 'I frolicked a little with the evidence.'

'This is chief inspector Joe of Scotland yard. We had a call for a possible murder. Oh, hello there, Isn't this

Mr William Joy. What're you doing here old lad? Seems like crimes follow you', cried the broad shouldered, white skinned, tall, and muscular inspector.

'It seems so my friend. There was, indeed, a murder, but unfortunately, the murderer jogged away before I had the opening of catching him.'

"'And thus, my dear Williams, I conclude the story requested by Abby to be written. I had a hard time writing this story. Tears kept falling every time I started to write. Her final request was that she could caution all the lovers she could with her story. I had to send you a copy of your own for, you perhaps should know, the other copy has its characters' names changed. We are till this day grateful for your actions. We gratify you till this day to our Lord; may he bless you.

"'With much affection, your dear, Ann.'"

Back in Baker Street, Williams lastly opened his eyes lids and gazed at the Landlord, 'Such a troublesome

adventure my dear Landlord. I shall never involve myself with lovers' affairs ever again', declared Williams as
he stood up and stretched his muscles.

'I have the same notion, sir. But who knows, as intel-
lectual and unemotional as you are, hearts may fall in

love without their masters' power.'

'Possibly my dear Landlord, possibly.'

'Oh. Wait, sir. I think there's still a slight paragraph on
the back. Shall I read it?' asked the Landlord.

'Pray, do so.'

'"I've made this story with her full account of events.
My sister was indeed schizophrenic as you have stated.
She was diagnosed with schizophrenia after her marriage
with a couple of months. Charles never gave up on her
even so. She began to suffer from heart complications
ever since the incident; thus, she spent most of her time
in the hospital. Her request was to publish this story
after her death. And as you've obviously deducted, she
passed away. Passed away this week... I shall always have
her on my mind. These are her last and final words:

'"**LOVE** is a pearl of purest hue,

But stormy waves are around it;

And dearly may a woman rue,

The hour that first, she found it."'

...END...

THE ADVENTURE OF OTHELLO'S DESPAIR
SUMMER I

Summer. Britain and summer. Salt and pepper. Life and death. Two concepts that don't quite have congruence amongst one another. Most people perceive summer as a sizzling sunny season, but not Britain's. In Britain, Williams seldom views the sun. Maybe on a couple of occasions and days, but most of the season he views the mushy white clouds with its vaporised water or at least in London it's this way.

'GREAT APOLLO!' murmured Williams Joy to himself as he opened the broad bow windows of his 221b flat. 'At last, some sun beams to light up my caved flat. This year's season is peculiar. Eh prefect?' uttered Williams in bewilderment as he turned to face the tall unemotional flat face of superintendent Parker of Scotland yard.

'Indeed, they're my dear Williams. Seems like this global warming thing that those up-to-date scientists gossip about is quite true. Hope it doesn't get worse while we're still around here', replied the superintendent with a titter as he watched Williams walking towards the turntable on the mantelpiece.

'You believe in that stuff, prefect? Didn't think you would do. Thought you hated modern scientists', said Williams as he searched through his vinyl records 'AHA!'

'Well, not necessarily. Found what you've been looking for?' asked the superintendent while observing Williams placing the vinyl on the turntable and placing the stylist over it.

'Indeed, I have. Vivaldi's Concerto No. 2 Op. 8. Yes, as you're deducing. Played this for this seldom occasional sunny seasonal day', replied Williams with ambition as he went back to the settee and the composition playing behind his back.

'One of his finest works. Quite Relatable for our season. But I prefer Chopin's nocturnes over him.'

'Chopin! Isn't as half as good as Beethoven. Lad's deaf and composed masterpieces. His works capture one's heart', replied Williams with hot-bloodedness.

'My dear friend, I'm not discrediting him. I just prefer the other. Anyhow, I see you've been wasting your life's time reading Shakespeare. I perceive the Othello play on your desk,' remarked the superintendent lifting the book off the desk and examining it.

'My life's been a boring one lately. No appealing cases lately. Wasting it with what I find.'

"And you waste it with Shakespeare's tragedies? The man's sadistic. Try some Marlowe. Will ya mate?"

'And quite the deviant. The human race now is as if its based-on love and the whole lot gyrates round it. Some people just don't understand that we can live off our lives without a lover', exclaimed Williams with an air of bewilderment and irritation towards homo sapiens.

'I perhaps have to agree on that point with the exception that life's not gonna be as full then or so I perceive. My objective is, if you live once, better live it to the fullest. Eh?'

'Life… why would people give meaning to it? Grief and anguish frame this earth and all we seem to think about is money and love. They don't quite observe the world from a bigger perspective. Every religious party lives with the concept that the world revolves around them. Anyhow, mayhap you're right, my dear superintendent. Better live it ignorant than knowledgeable and depressed.'

'In any case, now that we're mentioning Othello, today's gonna be held his play. Let us waste our lives and go. I know you don't like leaving your flat. Just think about it', suggested the superintendent with ambition. Williams turned his gaze towards the window for a few minutes then turned back towards the superintendent 'Perhaps you're right. I might get to see a first-class acting class!'

'It's agreed then. Let's meet in front of the Lyceum Theatre at quarter to 6', said the superintendent as he turned and walked towards the door to leave.

'Thee requisites remain remits!' replied Williams with a smile on his face.

Perhaps Shakespeare's labour is treasured by many, but not for Williams. He did not relish Williams Shakespeare's style of writing. Quite caustic having both the same name. Williams didn't tolerate Shakespeare's imagination and fancy words play. He thought that he complicated the beauty of the storyline with his fanciful words. Although his stories weren't that great, thought Williams, they were intolerable too. They were too stretched out. Hamlet is another play that Williams had ended this week with an exasperated look on his face for its stretched-out imagination. He did not comprehend why would anyone like his work and call it a magnum opus. Perhaps if you ask a man on the streets about Shakespeare, he'll reply by 'He's a symbol and a dazzling playwright.' If you ask them about his works, most of them will reply saying, 'Romeo and Juliet', or so thought Williams…

…

And as agreed on, at a quarter to 6, Williams was standing in front of the Lyceum Theatre waiting for the superintendent. A couple of minutes went by, and he saw the superintendent walking towards him. 'Off by a couple of minutes as always, superintendent', remarked Williams with a sigh.

'Apologise for that. You know me, my dear Williams. Anyhow, let's go in. The play's about to begin in any minute', replied the superintendent as they strolled towards the Theatre. They walked into the hall and ambled towards their seats 'By Jove! It already started,' cried the superintendent.

'Blame your carelessness, my dear prefect', replied Williams with a sigh.

Such a nice evening. To watch one of Shakespeare's plays, they thought. Was it going to be a nice evening? What Williams and the superintendent didn't have knowledge of at that time was the grotesque incident that was going to take place…

...

Time went by as they watched the play and they arrived at one of the ending scenes, of the story, where, apparently, Othello suffocates his wife, Desdemona, by thrusting a pillow upon her face and goes on to commit suicide afterwards by stabbing himself.

'Acting seems quite realistic, eh? Its as if he's lust went out of control and he's really murdering her', remarked the superintendent.

'Indeed, I quite agree. Acting is a first class one', replied Williams watching the play with attentiveness. The scene ended, and the curtains were closed for the preparation of the final scene. 'This was a pretty interesting scene. Actors were full of emotions', remarked the superintendent.

'Their acting was very decent. I must agree. At least it wasn't a waste coming here', replied Williams with a titter look towards the superintendent.

The minutes went by nonetheless, and the curtains were still closed. Perhaps 15 minutes went by, and the crowd waited. It's as if the play had ended and the crowd's waiting without an aim. Suddenly a gentleman appeared through the curtains. 'Please excuse our inconvenience, but, sorrowfully, an incident occurred with one of our workmates, and we have to close the play. Thank you for coming', and hurried mysteriously behind the curtains. The crowd began to have questions and ask each other 'What's the meaning of this.' 'Where's our money.' 'This is indeed an act of theft.' And so, the voices where raised and a commotion was made.

As luck would have it, a superintendent was present at the scene and took control of the situation professionally.

'IM SUPERINTENDENT PARKER OF SCOT-
LAND YARD. PLEASE KEEP CALM AND HAVE
YOUR THOUGHTS TO YOURSELVES. I'LL HAVE
A LOOK AT WHAT'S HAPPENING BEHIND.' And
so, the superintendent strolled through the curtains to
see what's taking place. Of course, behind him was Williams, eager as well to know what's taking place.

They got through the curtains and perceived two gath-
erings. One gathering of people was gathered around the
actor who acted as the character Desdemona and laid on
the ground, and the other gathering of people gathered
around the actor who acted as her husband, Othello.
There was a commotion amongst them. That was quite
observable. A voice began raise 'I DID NOOT DOO
IT! ARE YOU MAD CAP!?'

'PLEASE LOWER YOUR VOICES RIGHT NOW!
IM SUPERITEND PARKER OF SCOTLAND YARD.
WHAT HAS OCCURRED? WHAT IS WITH COM-
MOTION?' cried the superintendent with a voice so
fierce that you could've observed the veins starting to
pop up on his neck. The voices lowered, and all the people turned to the superintendent and observed him without saying a word. As if they're being hypnotised, just
gazing at the two men standing. The inspector observed
the lady on the ground and ran up to her, but to his
astonishment, he had already found Williams bending
beside the reddish haired exotic woman trying her pulse.
When did he leave his side, the superintendent didn't
know?

'Something wrong with her? Is she having a fever?'
asked the superintendent as he lowered beside the lady.

'I'm afraid she's dead. Died from chloroform over-exposure. Come closer to her face and try smelling her',

replied Williams turning his gaze from Desdemona to the superintendent.

"Chloroform!" cried the superintendent, expanding his eyes and looking towards Williams.

Was the thought that ran through the superintendent's mind, the same thought that ran through William's?

'Quite right! And from where you think it came from?'

'The pillow that Othello murdered her with!' cried that superintendent as he got up to observe all the actors surrounding him 'Where's the gent who played as Othello?' asked the superintendent looking around him.

'That was me, sir. Boot I tell you; I did not do it.' The voice came amongst the crowd, and a broad shouldered, tan skinned, built up man with a scar on his face stepped forward.

'Look here, young man. All the evidence aims towards you. I mean. Not just evidence, a hole troop of people observed you in the act.'

'I tell you man. I did not doo it. She wos me lover. How come I'll kill 'er. Don't be mad' cried the young man and stepped backwards. The superintendent observed him and sighed 'I pity you. For a reason, seem to believe your statement that you didn't intend to do it. I mean, it may have been an accident. You know, being too much engaged in the act and suffocating her without noticing. The judge may lower your sentence', said the superintendent while placing his hand on the young man's shoulder.

"Boot dis is madness. I did noot doo it. I DID NOOT KILL ME DEAR ELY!' cried the young man, and started to cry.

SUMMER I

'It's alright young man. I need all of you to know to hold your place and don't mess with the crime scene. Williams, I need you to call the ya…' 'Where did he go to?' asked the superintendent to himself as he observed that Williams had left the scene of the crime. 'Anyhow, who's in charge here?' asked the superintendent.

'That's got to be me, sir', said a voice. The superintendent turned his head to observe a short man with a beard on his face that without recognising his English accent, he would've thought that the man was Italian.

'What's your name, sir?' asked the superintendent.

'James T- sir. The director.'

'Alright, James. I need you sir to announce to the yard about this murder. Right now.'

'Understood, sir!' He turned and ran towards the closest phone station to ring for the yard.

...

A quarter of an hour, perhaps went by, and the yard was at the scene taking hold of the suspected butcher. Out of nowhere Williams appeared and took the superintendent by the arm. 'He's not our man. He did not kill her, I'm quite sure.' The superintendent was quite shocked to hear this statement. He just gazed at Williams 'Don't fret. I have a scheme, and I'm quite sure it will work.'

'But why. WHY isn't he our man? How come you're so sure?' asked the superintendent with eagerness.

'Maintain yourself and drop your voice. You don't want our convict's guard up. I'll explain once we've got him. Just do as I tell you…'

...

The yard took the known criminal away and so the actors were prepared to leave. 'It's been a disaster for our play! To our reputation!' were the whispers you heard amongst them. Williams and the superintendent were in a hideout. Each one in a particular hideout. Was this their scheme? To hide? Obviously waiting for someone, or something to happen. But what?

Williams sat in his hideout, thinking if his scheme is efficient. His hideout? Indeed? Where was he at? Where's this hideout. All dark except for the rows of light in front of him. Rows? Was he in a locker? What's he doing inside a locker? 'I'VE GOT HIM, MY DEAR WIL-LIAMS!' came the shouting voice of the superintendent from the other locker room 'WE'VE GOT THE MAN WHO MURDERED THE POOR LADY! PARDON ME! I MEANT TO SAY WE'VE GOT THE WOM-AN!' A woman! Williams got out of the locker to observe the identity of the criminal behind this devilish and grotesque murder. 'I suspected that you're the one behind this, Lady Mary.' Mary was apparently the actor who played Emilia, Iago's wife.

'HOW!? WHY! HOW DID YOU SUSPECT FOULPLAY!?' cried Emilia while trying to free herself from the superintendent's grip.

'Quite simple, rather' remarked Williams with a smirk.

'Indeed! Time for your explanation!' added the superintendent as he held on to Lady Mary tightly.

'Initially, my dear superintendent, when we observed the body, I remarked about the smell of chloroform on her face. When you gazed at me, I thought you got my object, but alas, another notion flashed through your mind. Your idea, obviously, was that Othello murdered the lady and chloroformed the pillow. But my dear superintendent, why would he need to add chloroform to the pillow?'

'Well, for murdering her more effortlessly', answered the superintendent with bewilderment.

'Quite obvious but… haven't you asked yourself why would a man this big and built up need chloroform to strangle a lady that's barley half his size? If he wanted to strangle her, he wouldn't need chloroform. Or if he needed, he wouldn't use this much to give him away. But then again, if he wanted to strangle her deliberately, why would a sane man, in the name of heavens and Apollo, strangle her in front of a thousand people!?'

There was silence in the air. No one uttered a word. If there was a fly, you could've heard its sound clearly.

'Anyhow, after apprehending that, the real criminal placed a large dosage of chloroform in the pillow so that with the applied force by Othello, she would surely die of chloroform over-exposure and strangulation. I have to say, it's quite ingenious. Nevertheless, I searched the crime scene for the pillow that was used for the crime. I know what you're thinking. Indeed, it wasn't at the crime scene, so someone had to take it and hide it. There wasn't much time for our suspected criminal to get rid of the pillow, so he had to hide it somewhere safe for the moment and then dispose of it later on. While you were cross-examining the actors, I busied myself searching for the pillow, but, alas, didn't find it anywhere till I passed by the locker rooms. Of course, it must have been hidden in the safest place possible! A locker where no one can open it except the murderer himself. The problem was that I didn't know if the pillow was in the men's or women's locker room, so I had a scheme.

My scheme was that I would lower your guard down by making Othello the official murderer and each one of us, the superintendent and I, hid in a locker room and waited for our prey to come to us instead of the opposite', explained Williams, lastly.

'Now that you explain it, it seems quite simple. I was such half-witted. Such an obvious fact! How didn't I notice', cried the superintendent with a furious face upon his face. Lady Mary was silent. She only gazed on the ground, 'you said you suspect me of the act. Why?' she asked, raising her head to look at Williams.

'Well, it was a hunch perhaps. When the superintendent was questioning everyone after the incident, everyone was looking at Othello with a face that showed either anger or indifference. Only you... only you had that look that showed hatred and satisfaction. The clinching of your right fist and a little unobservable smirk. I didn't know if you were the suspected murderer or you just possessed pure hatred towards the fellow. What I know is... he may have been your lover in the past. Why then all this hatred towards an acquaintance? Am I right?' asked Williams lastly.

'I WAS ENGAGED TO HIM TILL THAT GOOD FOR NOTHING WOMAN CAME IN-BETWEEN OUR LIVES AND RUINED EVERYTHING. EVERYTHING!' cried lady Mary as she bent down to her knees and started sobbing.

III

Back in 221b the morning of the next day, Williams was sitting on his desk observing a letter he was holding from superintendent Parker. 'We barely left each other a couple of hours ago. What's on his mind now? Perhaps another case!' With that thought on his mind, thence Williams opened the letter hurriedly, but alas, it wasn't a new case. It was just the superintendent being his normal self...

"'Dear Williams,

"I have thought about our conversation that took place in your flat yesterday and our little adventure we had afterwards. I have come to this conclusion; love, hatred, jealousy, or sentiments are mostly the reasons why humans don't advance as a species. It's our ruin. Our defect. It causes depression, hatred, and mostly murderers, at least it keeps our jobs working.

"I know it isn't a laughing matter, but as a human, I came to realise your words that we need to control our emotions. We're nothing but mere species. The person you think is the one for you may not be if it wasn't for the chance of you seeing him. Yes, chance! So why do we care so much about them? Mere strangers entering our lives and being that important. I perhaps think that sentiments are a chemical defect in our human brain. Although I have this question on my mind… Is it possible for humans to live in harmony although they lack emotions?

-Your dearest Parker D.'"

…END…

SUPPORT THE AUTHOR:

I self-publish privately, therefore, anyone, if interested, can support me and check out my services on my website:

www.amirjoy.net.

PICTURE CREDITS:

All pictures and images are supplied and
illustrated by the author.
Flat A221b illustrated by Mr Russel Stuber.